"I want to know everything there is about you."

She gave a nervous laugh. "You know, so I can get a full picture of the man I'm working with."

"Working with?" he asked with the raise of a brow.

"Just tell me what you need in a relationship."

He hadn't said he *needed* anything, merely what he believed was an indicator, but he didn't correct her. "I think if you are dating the right person, they will help you be the best version of yourself. They will push you to your next level. Together, you should feel like you can take on the world. If they are holding you back, in any way—" as he spoke those words, he felt a tug at his heart that told him this was probably him when it came to her "—then you should find someone better."

There was a look of pain in her expression. "Well, I'm glad we don't have to worry about anything like that," she said, turning away.

LONE WOLF BOUNTY HUNTER

DANICA WINTERS

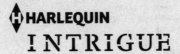

To my family, friends and fans.

May this and all of my books help bring light to the darkness.

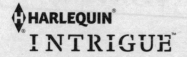

ISBN-13: 978-1-335-58212-6

Lone Wolf Bounty Hunter

Copyright © 2022 by Danica Winters

Recycling programs for this product may not exist in your area.

For questions and comments about the quality of this book, please contact us at CustomerService@Harlequin.com.

Harlequin Enterprises ULC
22 Adelaide St. West, 41st Floor
Toronto, Ontario M5H 4E3, Canada
www.Harlequin.com

Printed in U.S.A.

Danica Winters is a multiple-award-winning, bestselling author who writes books that grip readers with their ability to drive emotion through suspense and occasionally a touch of magic. When she's not working, she can be found in the wilds of Montana, testing her patience while she tries to hone her skills at various crafts—quilting, pottery and painting are not her areas of expertise. She believes the cup is neither half-full nor half-empty, but it better be filled with wine. Visit her website at danicawinters.net.

Books by Danica Winters

Harlequin Intrigue

STEALTH: Shadow Team

A Loaded Question
Rescue Mission: Secret Child
A Judge's Secrets
K-9 Recovery
Lone Wolf Bounty Hunter

Stealth

Hidden Truth
In His Sights
Her Assassin For Hire
Protective Operation

Mystery Christmas

Ms. Calculation
Mr. Serious
Mr. Taken
Ms. Demeanor

Smoke and Ashes
Dust Up with the Detective
Wild Montana

Visit the Author Profile page at Harlequin.com.

CAST OF CHARACTERS

Kendra Spade—A prosecutor from New York whose family runs STEALTH, a military contracting and private security company that is at odds with a Montana state senator. When called to action to defend her family, she must face the pain of her past and find hope for her future.

Trent Lockwood—The co-owner of Lockwood Bonds and a man who prides himself on his ability to do the right thing in a world that seems to focus on everything that is wrong.

Tripp Lockwood—Fellow co-owner of the family business, Trent's older brother and a man who is known to be an acquired taste.

AJ Spade—Kendra's older brother and a man who thinks his primary objective is to make her come to the family's heel.

Senator Dean Clark—A man with an ego as large as any cowboy's belt buckle. Awaiting trial for his role in his wife's murder and daughter's kidnapping, he files a lawsuit against the Spades with the goal of turning the public's perception of guilt from him to the shadow team.

Brad Bradshaw—A criminal defense attorney and the head of the Bradshaw Law Group, a firm that is working to defend the senator with the hope it will be a feather in their caps and a boon for their company.

Marla Thomas—The cosigner for the senator's bond at the Lockwoods' shop. Though she should be easy to track down, she is the hardest of all thanks to her masked truths and open lies.

Chapter One

It was a gift, nearly dying. After a lifetime spent on the front lines of her family's many wars, it wasn't until she was wounded and feared dead that she finally found herself with the freedom to really live.

The wound under her left clavicle was Kendra Spade's daily reminder of how close she had come to the edge. Yet it had also been her get-out-of-the-family-business-free card. It was a bullet that she would have gladly taken again.

She slipped on her silk shirt and buttoned it, leaving the top open to expose the diamond solitaire necklace that adorned the base of her throat. Like any shiny thing, it had a way of attracting the biggest fish and the widest mouths. Judge Giuseppe always commented on her necklace after the hearings. She held no doubts, thanks to the look in his evil-dulled eyes, that it wasn't only the necklace he found beautiful. That being said, she would never be the kind of woman who would sell her soul for a judge's favor—there were far better and easier ways to get what she wanted.

She picked up her suit jacket, laid it over her arm and slipped on her blood-bottomed heels. Before walking out of her office, she put on her lipstick and checked her lines in the mirror by the door—as always, she appeared picture-perfect.

It was a good thing the looking glass wasn't capable of peeking into her soul. If it was, it would see all the struggles that came with being a prosecutor and a woman with a past. Everything in her life was peppered with wounds and emotional shrapnel, but the best part of it was the scars—they were the body's way of fusing itself and its weaknesses into a stronger and more resilient space.

She touched the puckered place under her clavicle for good luck and picked up her briefcase. This would be a tough case, but if things went her way—which they usually did—she wouldn't need any luck, just the power of her research and her persuasion. Today was just a bench trial, so she would only have to convince Judge Giuseppe that the defendant had committed the murder he was charged with, and that it was premeditated, not an act of self-defense. The defense had taken a risk, going for a bench trial instead of asking for a jury, and she was all too happy to oblige. Judge Giuseppe was fair and consistent on the law. Juries could be capricious.

The trial would likely last the rest of the afternoon, but it would be dollars in her pocket—money that allowed her to be almost completely free of her ties with her family's private security company, STEALTH. They regularly worked as military contractors and had operatives all over the world, including several right here in New York.

On second thought, she would never be truly free.

Her phone buzzed as she walked up the courthouse steps, and she slipped it out of her briefcase—AJ.

Speak of the devil.

She considered not answering and letting the phone call go to voicemail, but her brother would just keep calling until she did pick up—and that was to say nothing of the rest of the family that he would call to the table and ask to reach out to her as well. They were wolves when they needed to be, and she would always be called back to the pack when pride or lives were at stake.

"AJ." She said his name simply, affectless.

"Glad to catch you. You busy?"

He knew the answer to that question. She was always busy—just like him. "Not too bad. You?"

"Just another day in paradise." AJ chuckled. "I don't know what you've heard about the ranch we're working from in Montana, but we have a situation on our hands."

She could feel a request coming on the flotsam of his words, and she wasn't sure if she wanted to go in for the direct hit and get it over with or if she should make him work for the ask—either way, she would be urged to do his bidding. First, she needed to know if this call to action was because of imminent danger to person or pride.

"What happened?" she asked.

AJ exhaled. "We've had a run-in with a state senator whom we were hired by. He admitted to having his wife killed and his child kidnapped, but now he has recanted and told us that he was coerced into his testimony and feared that STEALTH would kill him if he didn't take the blame."

So, this threat had the bite of both injury of pride and death of souls. "And now he is suing the family?"

"And you knowing that is exactly why we need you to come home and work on our behalf."

"You know as well as I do that I'm not licensed in Montana. I'd be of little to no help. However, I can make a few calls and get you the best lawyer possible."

"No," AJ said, his tone making it clear that there was no argument she could make that would grant her reprieve from his request. "You are the best lawyer I know and the only one we can truly trust. And, if you look, you will notice that you actually *are* licensed in the State of Montana. You can thank Zoey for that one when you get here."

"Just because you had your team…" She glanced around, making sure that no one was listening in on her conversation, but everyone around her kept moving and seemed wrapped up in their own lives. "Just because you *hacked* the state bar and faked documents, it doesn't mean that I will step into line with your plans. What you did is unethical, and if anyone was to find out, I'd be permanently disbarred."

AJ sighed. "The only one who has the power, or could find the proof to get you disbarred, would be you."

She held no doubts he was right—their boss, Zoey, would have done everything in triplicate and spared no expense to sell their ruse. Yet it didn't change the fact she wasn't acquainted with the intricacies of the Montana state legal system and its statutes.

"You've put my reputation, my credibility and my honor at stake, and now you want me to do you a favor? I don't like being strong-armed, AJ," she growled.

"And yet you are still talking to me. We both know that you love me and your family. We have you booked on a flight out this afternoon. All you have to do is go and present your case in front of Giuseppe and secure the guilty verdict that we both know you will get—then go to JFK. We have everything else you will need when you get here."

Damn, they've done their research.

She might have hated being pushed around by her brother, but he was also the only one she loved enough to allow him to get away with treating her like a child despite the fact that she'd grown into a strong, independent woman. No matter how powerful she became or how far she tried to push her family from her world, all he had to do was make a call and prove that he would always have sway—but his most influential weapon to bring her to heel was her love for him and her other siblings. Family would always come first.

"I'll see you tonight," he said, almost as if he could hear the thoughts and the arguments she was having within herself.

"There had better be whiskey and fresh ice in my bedroom when I arrive."

Maybe the only time she would ever truly be free would be when she broke the chains of love she felt for her family—but death would wield that ax, something she didn't want for any of them. Until then, when they pulled the chains tight, she had no choice but to do their bidding.

GETTING GIUSEPPE TO issue the right verdict had been fairly straightforward. A handful of hours later, she found herself seated in a puddle jumper and flying from Minneapolis into Missoula. At least her family had the good sense to book her first-class, but that meant little on the tiny airplane. Basically, she got one extra bag of pretzels and was the first one in line for the cheese tray.

After boarding, she clicked her seat belt in place,

and an auburn-haired man with piercing brown eyes smiled down at her. He was wearing cowboy boots, jeans and what she could best describe as something that had come off a ranch supplier's discount rack— though he made that Western-style shirt look good.

"Hey," he said, giving her a nod before stowing his black backpack in the overhead compartment and sitting down.

She gave him a tip of the head and a tight-lipped smile as he clicked in. If she had any luck, that would be where their conversation ended. She didn't mind a little chitchat on a flight, but she didn't like being cloistered next to such a good-looking man for that length of time—actually, any length of time. And this man was definitely good-looking. He had deep-set eyes and the brooding scowl of a thoughtful and intrepid soul.

He glanced over at her, and his eyes picked up the light from her window, making them shine the color of warm caramel. She doubted any woman who'd looked into those eyes had ever felt the ability to say no to any kind of request he made. He was definitely the kind who had his fair share of options when it came to women—and she wasn't the kind who wanted to compete for any man's attention. She commanded respect and, above all, loyalty.

The plane steadily filled with college students, smiling couples and single professionals. She glanced down at her phone. She hadn't even put it on airplane mode yet, and she already had twenty new emails from her office and her clients. While waiting for the flight, she had taken care of what she could and made a few brief phone calls, but her thoughts returned to AJ. He hadn't told her much about what the senator was threatening to do to her family and STEALTH, the private military contracting company that employed them. Well, all except her…for the last few years. *It was a nice reprieve while it lasted.*

"Ma'am?" a flight attendant asked. She hadn't noticed he was standing in the aisle and looking down at her, and his sudden appearance made her jump with surprise.

"Yes?" she asked, her cheeks warming with the thought she had been caught unaware.

"Can you please push your purse farther under your seat?" He motioned toward her leather bag, which was barely showing and, if she had been given a choice, would have never been on the floor in the first place.

She forced a smile, clicked off her phone and dropped it into her bag before reaching to push it deeper under the seat. She felt a snap and her fingernail snagged on the man's bag that was on the floor next to hers, but she barely paid attention as she finished shoving the bag under her seat and sat back up.

The steward didn't crack a smile and moved his way down the aisle, doing his best impersonation of an overworked schoolmarm in the process—she was surprised he didn't have a ruler to rap on flyers who ignored or failed to comply to his standards.

The man next to her cleared his throat. "If you'd like, I can put your bag in the overhead compartment for you."

"Thank you for the offer, but it's fine." And just like that, she'd had enough of men for the day. The last thing she was going to do was hand her purse over to the care of a stranger so he could put it out of her sight.

A sigh escaped her lips before she had a chance to check the sound.

She could feel the gaze of the man sitting next to her; he must have picked up on her unspoken annoyance. "I am sorry," she said, not bothering to try to deny her actions. "I have had a long day, and it's not even close to ending."

The plane rolled back and taxied out onto the runway, getting in line for takeoff.

The man beside her smiled, his teeth as gleaming and beautiful as his eyes. "You're fine. I get that way, too. Where are you flying out of, originally?"

Her fears of chitchatting were being realized, and she only had herself to blame. It was a good thing her legal cases didn't usually hinge on a single sigh; sometimes she found it only too hard to keep her body language in check.

"New York City." She left it simple, not wanting to have the man continue with his line of questions.

He nodded, pinching his lips together as if he had more that he wanted to ask her but had picked up her reticence. "I'm coming from there as well. Funny, we might have been on the last plane together, too."

His words were innocuous, but something about the way he spoke made the hair on the back of her neck rise.

She turned to him, facing him carefully and searching his eyes for some kind of recognition, but she found nothing but the features of the handsome stranger. "Do I know you?"

He smiled, closed his eyes and let the G-force press his head back against the seat as they took off, forcing her retreat back to her headrest as well.

As the plane leveled out, she had the plummeting feeling that this man was a plant. He could play coy, but she wouldn't put it past her brother to put a tail on her to ensure she made it on the plane and safely to Montana.

He didn't say another word. He seemed to be asleep in the seat next to her—effectively trapping her. Ten minutes ago, she had hoped the man wouldn't talk to her, and now that her wish had come true, she was wishing for exactly the opposite—and to find out if her intuition was right or if she was simply losing her edge.

She battled with herself as she occasionally glanced over at him throughout the three-hour flight. When the surly flight attendant returned with the cart, she hoped the man would stir, but instead the attendant passed him over and gave her the little box of snacks and three minibottles of vodka—two of which she would definitely need to save for later.

After downing the first minibottle, she looked over at the sleeping man. His chin was tilted back, but even in sleep he was sexy. This man, this stranger next to her, was just that—a stranger.

If she was already having to worry about intrigues and plots her family was involved in before her feet even struck ground in Montana, this was going to be one hell of a trip—a trip she would have to work hard to cut short.

Chapter Two

Trent Lockwood could have murdered his assistant for seating him beside their target. She knew his policy—always stick to the shadows—and yet his twenty-four-year-old secretary at Lockwood Bonds had gone ahead and broken the rules. As soon as he got back to Missoula, she would get a talking-to about what exactly it meant for him to be a bonds-man and bounty hunter—and the danger that came with his job.

He peeked out from under his eyelashes at the lawyer sitting next to him. She was pretty—prettier than he had expected, based on the pictures he had picked up of her online. In real life, her blond curls were looser and free-flowing around her hard-edged jawline and supple pink cheeks, and they almost worked to conceal the way she occasionally looked over at him.

Did she sense something in him? Or was she just as leery of strangers as he was? People were the most dangerous weapons in the world, and he was only too sure she knew this fact just as well as he did.

He couldn't read too much into her sizing him up. Hell, maybe she was just as bored as he was. He'd been hoping to use this time to catch up on some recon on Senator Clark and his whereabouts, but instead here he was…being scrutinized by the one person he had hoped to never be noticed by. Rather, he hoped she would lead him to the man who had left his company on the hook for a million-dollar bond—a bail bond his brother had signed off on in desperation to make money. Trent had only come to terms with it when Tripp had finally convinced him it was a benefit to have a senator as a client.

Yes, he would definitely need to call a team meeting about expectations and job requirements the moment he got back. As for his seat assignment, it would have to result in a formal write-up of the secretary, if nothing else. She shouldn't make these kinds of mistakes when lives were on the line.

He couldn't have been more relieved when they touched down. Hopefully he had been utterly forgettable. The last thing he needed was her recognizing him outside this airplane. Most women he had met over the years had been only too happy to forget him; he'd never been great at the relationship game. That kind of thing was for people who didn't have to live half of their lives ducking in and out of alleys. As a professional bounty hunter, he lived on the edge of danger every day.

Trent had only been with his last girlfriend for a few months before she kicked him to the curb after he disappeared for a week—four days longer than he was supposed to have been gone. Though he had tried to explain it was for work, he hadn't had the heart to lie to her when she asked how often that kind of thing happened—far too often. It had also contributed to his divorce prior to that, but his ex had bottled up her questions and concerns until it was too late to save the marriage.

Trent was damned good at his job, but that was because he had the patience to wait—a personality trait that didn't work so well when it came to burgeoning relationships in the digital and instant-gratification age. The best thing about his job was the hunt. He could take his time and watch the people he was sent to bring to heel—the people who left his family's company holding the bag when they failed to show up for court and jumped bail.

After landing, he made his way out to his rental truck, carefully keeping an eye on Kendra. From what he'd managed to hear from the grapevine, Kendra was coming to town to sit down and have a closed-door mediation with the senator and his lawyers at the Bradshaw Law offices. He had been sitting on that lawyer's office for nearly a month, and so far come up empty-handed. Hopefully, Kendra's meeting would prove to be as fruitful as they expected, but it meant not losing track of her.

She got into a white Suburban parked just outside the terminal. A man greeted her; he was about six feet and the kind that looked like he worked out at least five times a week. Trent gritted his teeth, and as he caught himself doing it, he wondered why. Kendra was pretty, but what in the hell was he doing being even the slightest bit annoyed about a stranger helping someone who was little more than bait for his intended target?

Sure, she was pretty...*stunningly beautiful*, if he was being honest with himself. Yet he couldn't be, nor was he the type to be, smitten with a woman simply because of her looks. As far as he was concerned, beauty on the outside was a depreciating asset. The only thing that he really looked for in a woman he considered dating was a soul that could speak to him in the night without a word ever being whispered.

He pulled his truck around, keeping his eye on her Suburban. After paying for his parking, he followed her out onto the main road, carefully keeping at least three car lengths behind. Her destination was a mystery; there had been no records of her at any of the local hotels, and he couldn't find anything about the physical location of the company she was representing in the lawsuit, STEALTH Inc.

He wasn't a tech guru by any means, but he'd put in more than his fair share of time in the tech trenches, and he knew how to locate people based on a variety of methods and using a variety of tools—many utilized by law enforcement. Yet he had come up with nothing about this woman besides generic work info and a professional headshot; she was an enigma when it came to her personal life. He'd be lying to himself if he didn't admit that her ability to hide in this world was a bit of a turn-on.

The thought made him fall back slightly more into the mass of traffic after leaving the lot. If her digital protections were that strong, he could only imagine her physical ones were just as robust—ones that would definitely include watching for tails and men who wished to be utterly forgettable.

After driving for nearly forty-five minutes, carefully keeping his distance the entire time, the white Suburban turned off and onto a dirt road that led toward a gulch tucked into the belly of the mountains. The road was barely marked, and he dropped a pin on his map to make sure he could find it again later.

He drove past and didn't stop until he hit the small town of Stevensville, not much farther down the road. The town was little more than it had been 150 years ago—comprised of a couple bars, a post office and a bank. In fact, the brick facades of the main street seemed straight out of the 1880s, complete with flat roofs and the lawless feel of the old West.

He'd grown up around western Montana, but it never ceased to amaze him when he came into these small towns how much they gripped the past and generational pride.

No matter what came in his life, he would always be pulled back to this world—a simpler place in a simpler time.

Parking his truck, Trent went to work. According to OnX, a mapping app, the road she had driven down led to a four-hundred-acre ranch called the Widow Maker. It had been bought and sold a few years back, and it was registered under a private holding company's name. *That clever woman.*

There were no guarantees that this was the STEALTH headquarters, but his sixth sense was kicking into high gear. Ranches were often kept in trusts or overseen by private holding companies, depending on the size and the owners' desire for privacy, but if he had to guess, this was exactly where he needed to go in order to keep a line on her.

He glanced back at his phone. It would be dark, pitch-dark, in about an hour. He'd have to be vigilant, but as soon as he got what he needed, he could retreat into the shadows. If he had only known they were going to be seated next to one another on the plane, he could have planted a tracker directly on her gear, but instead he was stuck playing a nighttime spy.

From what he'd managed to pull up about STEALTH, they were a private military contracting group…that much he knew. Yet, aside from organizations like Blackwater, he had heard very little of what businesses like this actually did. Blackwater had developed a reputation for skirting the law, killing innocent people and generally leaving chaos in their wake, but he had a feeling that STEALTH wasn't the kind of team that worked at that level. Though he could be wrong.

He pulled up his VPN and started searching for more information. Unlike Blackwater, STEALTH had nothing about them online aside from a monochromatic website that touted their security services—he'd pored through their website before, but it had given him about as few answers as the woman who had been seated next to him.

Closing his eyes for a moment, he was surprised when her face popped into the front of his mind. Had he really looked at her so long that her image had imprinted on him like that? Or was she there because he was paid to have her be his every thought?

It had to be the latter.

He needed to get to the water; that was the only way he could make sense of what he was thinking and feeling—and maybe it would grant him the peace that he so desperately sought. Ever since his divorce, he'd found being on the water the therapy he needed to find tranquility again. The river was silent and nonjudgmental. His ex had been silent and critical.

Glancing back at the map, he noted the river that twisted through STEALTH's property. In Montana, rivers and riverbanks were public property—and damn if he wasn't a member of the public. He smiled.

It was the perfect time for fishing when he got on the river. The sun was a finger's width from touching the top of the mountains that surrounded him, and its golden and pink hues were reflecting off the water. He pulled a caddis fly from his kit and lathered it up with floatant.

There was nothing like fishing with dry flies. An angler had to make them dance just over the surface of the water to lure the trout from the depths, then lace the fly onto the water and wait for the hungry fish to rise. It was the ultimate game of seduction.

He made his way down the riverbank until he was well within the boundaries of the ranch, but he was careful to stay as concealed as possible. Occasionally, he would throw a cast and wait for a strike, but mostly he watched. In the distance, he could make out a line of cabins, like little row houses, where he assumed the ranch hands would have lived, but in this case they were far more likely to be housing trained spies and killers.

It made him wonder about Kendra. Was she a killer? A spy?

If she was, there was no way he was getting the drop on her.

The thought made his skin prickle, and he couldn't help but look over his shoulder. Just because no one had come out and given him the once-over, it didn't mean they didn't know he was here. No one stood behind him, but he looked to the trees, already convinced that he would find cameras pinned on him. Once again, there was nothing.

A woman stepped out of one of the cabins nearest him. He cast his line, looking at her only from his peripheral. She stood, watching him, for a long moment. She was far enough away that he couldn't make out her features, but even without seeing them, he knew it was her... Kendra.

A part of him hoped that she would walk toward the river...that she would walk to him, put her hand to his cheek and say, "I've been hoping to see you again."

She turned away from him, and he found solace in her ignoring him. If she had recognized him, she likely would have confronted him...especially if she was actually a trained mercenary. She wouldn't just shrug him off. Apparently, she was every bit a lawyer.

He watched her walk up the hill and toward the main ranch house until she disappeared. With her absence, a strange and unwelcome loneliness filled him, but he reminded himself the sensation was nothing more than his desire to do his job. That was all she was, a job. He needed to push aside all the superfluous feelings. This woman was all that stood between his family and potential ruin—and he could never let his heart get in the way of their business.

Chapter Three

"AJ, you know you can be a real son of a—" Kendra stopped as the house's front door slammed shut. She'd been home only a day, and they were already yelling at each other. She shouldn't have been surprised, but she was still disappointed.

"All I'm saying is that I think it best if you have a sit-down with the opposing counsel. Maybe we can sort something out before we take this to court and it all goes on the public record. Mediation would be the smartest route here," AJ argued. The water glass in his hand shook, and a bit sloshed over the top as he seemed to forget he was holding anything.

"I came here, against my better judgment, because you wanted the big guns. Now you want me to negotiate? I could have done that over the phone, sitting in my comfortable leather chair in my office in New York."

"I didn't think that they would be game for a sit-down until this morning," AJ countered. "I'd offered before, but they didn't even call me back."

"And yet, they just randomly called you after I hit the state? You are full of crap and you know it. You knew the whole time the mediation would happen—that's why you were in a mad rush to get me back here in time." She was so furious that she could feel her blood pressure rising all the way into her fingertips. "You know, I always tell my clients there are a lot of things I can do to help people, but the one thing I require in order to be able to do my job is the truth."

"I am *telling* you the damned truth, Kendra. You just aren't listening."

Oh, no, he didn't. She seethed.

There was the sound of laughter from outside the front door, then the latch clicked and Mike and Troy walked inside. Mike stopped, and his face went blank as he looked at her. He stared for a long moment, like he almost didn't recognize her. "Holy crap, look what the cat dragged in. When did you get here, sis?"

She shot AJ a look, making it clear their conversation was far from being over. He was going to get more of an earful about his bringing her here and then putting her in a holding pattern before she would be satisfied. "Hey, guys," she said, sighing as she struggled to gain control over her rage.

Troy walked over and gave her a quick kiss to the cheek. "I heard you might be coming back to town but didn't know you would be here so soon. Good to see you. You're looking…" He appraised her tailored pants and formfitting button-down. "Well, you look *New York*–ish."

She gave him a raise of the brow. "You know, not everyone in the world gets to wear tactical gear and hiking clothes for their day jobs. Some of us are expected to look and *act* professional." She glared over at AJ one more time, making sure he heard the admonishment in her tone.

He wouldn't glance her way. "I hate to cut this little reunion short, but we have places to be." AJ smiled. "And so do you. The Bradshaw Law Group office is a thirty-minute drive." He threw her a set of keys. "You can use the ranch truck as much as you need, but keep it between the mustard and the mayonnaise. I know how you drive."

First, he had the audacity to give her orders and push her around, and now he was going to comment on her driving? She could feel her lip curl with disgust as she caught the keys and stuffed them in her pocket.

Though she knew it was likely in vain, she tried to tell herself that AJ's attitude toward her was more a reflection of his love than it was his annoyance. He was just a leader, a typical type-A guy, and with that came traits that were sometimes hard to digest. Though, admittedly, she had that personality type as well.

She'd had more than her fair share of run-ins with her fellow state employees because of her inability to compromise or give any slack when she felt people weren't living up to their potential and doing as she had instructed. There was nothing she had less patience for than a person who ignored her, especially when it came to running a business and practicing law.

Maybe AJ was feeling the same way with her right now.

Logically, she could make sense of all this, but it was like being around her brother—and the rest of her family, for that matter—made her instantly become an eighteen-year-old girl again. Regardless of how much she wanted to fall into the trap of an identity crisis, she didn't have time for that. She could do that when she got back to New York into the safety of her own apartment. The longer she stayed in Montana, the more of a problem this would become, and she wasn't the kind to deal with her own personal drama well.

She turned to Mike and Troy and gave them a tip of the head. Mike smiled, like he knew this was about as close to her saying "I love you" as she would ever get. She wasn't the mushy, gushy kind. "I'll be back later this evening. If you don't mind, would you fit AJ with a ball gag before I get back?" She laughed.

Troy snorted.

"I'm not getting that close to his mouth. After the show you just put on with him, he's likely to bite."

Mike chuckled as he opened the door. "Your ranch truck carriage awaits, my lady."

Apparently, all her siblings were looking for a fight. At least she knew Mike was kidding. Regardless, this would be one hell of a long trip.

IT HAD BEEN a while since she had been behind the wheel of a truck, but it didn't take her long to get back into the swing of things. Thankfully, it wasn't a manual transmission or she would have never made it out of the driveway. She definitely wouldn't put it past AJ to stick her with one just to make her look stupid and keep the hierarchy between the two of them clear—he was boss and she was just one of his minions.

Maybe if she handled this meeting well, she could get out of the state by the end of the day.

In negotiations like this, it was always just about finding what was motivating the other party and then capitalizing on personal weaknesses. There was something brutal about it, but that savagery and the ability to go after blood was what had made her an effective lawyer in New York. The attorneys she fought against were sharks. Any scent of blood in the water, and not only would that shark feed upon her, but all the rest would as well.

So far, the best defense she had found against sharks was being the biggest one in the ocean.

She pulled up to the Bradshaw Law office and

noticed a dark-colored rental truck driving by the parking lot. She didn't know why it caught her attention, but something about it made the hair on the back of her neck stand at attention. Though she was sure it was just her being back here that was making her paranoid, she'd long ago learned to respect her body's innate intuition. It probably had nothing to do with the truck, but she needed to pay attention.

First, she needed to get her act together. The fates always favored those prepared. No doubt, the Bradshaw Group had received the court filing notifying them she had taken on the case. Which meant they had been doing hours of research on her before she would ever set foot in that office. Aside from the little bit of research she had done this morning and what AJ had told her about the case, she'd not gotten much and hadn't had time to do the level of digging she required.

In the middle of chastising herself, her phone pinged with an email from Zoey, the leader of the STEALTH team. Clicking on it, she wondered if Zoey could read her mind. The email itself was simple: Thought you might need this. Good luck.

Attached was an encrypted dossier on the Bradshaw Law Group, Senator Dean Clark and the lawsuit they had filed against STEALTH.

Most of what Zoey had provided was low-level dirt, the kind anyone could find with a little bit of searching around on the internet. Kendra also knew the senator had jumped bail, missing a preliminary hearing on his trial. The rat was so confident of public approval, he obviously didn't feel the need to abide by the rules. Lucky for her family, this would make defending the defamation lawsuit a little easier.

Kendra needed more information. However, if she played her cards right, the other counselor would give her everything she needed. She'd like to hope she'd get lucky, but over the last few days, luck certainly hadn't seemed to be on her side.

Out of the corner of her eye, she noticed the same dark truck as before, pulling into the parking lot across the street from her. The area was a large industrial complex with a variety of office buildings, but once again she found herself prickling.

She reached down for her purse, making sure that her concealed carry was in place. With a job like hers, she always had enemies. Every so often, ghosts from her past cases would float into her life and haunt her. It didn't seem likely that here in the middle of nowhere Montana one of her ghosts would find her, but complacency was a lawyer's worst enemy.

She stepped out of her truck, keeping her hand on her concealed carry inside her purse, looking as though she was digging around for ChapStick or some other irrelevant item, but she made sure to keep her eyes on the truck.

She couldn't see through the truck's tinted windows, and the realization brought her no comfort.

She picked up her pace and hurried into the building, not stopping until she was safely masked by a stairwell leading up. She stopped behind what limited cover there was and looked out. A man in a pair of jeans and a long-sleeve shirt had gotten out, but his back was to her and she couldn't see his face. More than likely, he was just another lawyer going to one of the offices across the street or something.

She was losing her mind.

Maybe this was what she got for trying to trust her instincts. Maybe this level of paranoia had simply been set in motion thanks to AJ and her family. It was really no wonder—every time she was around them, something bad happened.

She gave a long exhale and turned away from the man in the jeans. Something about him reminded her of the guy from the airplane yesterday.

Maybe if she had just talked to the guy on the plane, or made idle chitchat with anyone, she wouldn't be as paranoid as she was feeling right now. Maybe she had needed a single-serving friend to come to take the edge off. Oh well—now it was too late to worry about things like that. Now she needed to put her game face on.

I am the shark.

According to the sign in the main lobby, the Bradshaw Law Group took up the entirety of the third floor. They definitely weren't a fly-by-night firm. They were making enough in the small town to pay for an entire floor in an upscale neighborhood. Not only that, but it said something that Senator Dean Clark was one of their clients.

Having his case was a feather in any law firm's cap, and undoubtedly they would pull no punches and stop at nothing to make sure he got whatever it was that he wanted. In this case, he wanted to take her family down. No matter what, that wasn't going to happen.

She'd faced tougher adversaries in and out of the courtroom than this man hell-bent on revenge. According to what she'd been sent, he was upset after his wife had been murdered and his daughter had been kidnapped—according to the news, he had allegedly been behind the abductions in hopes of swaying public favor to help him get reelected. As such, he had a criminal case pending for his role in kidnapping, which had led to his wife's death and led to him losing custody of his daughter—permanently. Even with those marks against him, he had won his reelection campaign.

When STEALTH had been in control of the daughter's personal security, they'd had very limited control over the family's movements, only tasked with watching the girl outside the home and when and if the wife asked them to do so beyond that. According to the protocol and the contracts between STEALTH and the family, they had done everything by the book.

In fact, she would go so far as to say they had gone above and beyond the call of duty in helping search for the daughter and the wife as well as playing an integral role in bringing the killer down…and learning the senator himself was complicit in the kidnapping. It was the senator's malfeasance that had gotten him in this hot water. This lawsuit was nothing more than some trumped-up malarkey to make it appear STEALTH and her family were inept and had some sort of vendetta against the senator—though nothing could have been further from the truth.

Once again, the senator was just posturing. It seemed to be the only thing he was good at.

He probably wouldn't even be in the office today. If she was sitting on the opposite side of the courtroom on this one, she would've told him to stay as far away from this meeting as possible. It was all about grandstanding and playing head games.

As she reached the third floor, she straightened her blouse and ran a hand over her hair to make sure every strand was in place in her no-nonsense bun. The best defense was a strong offense.

Game on.

She allowed her heart rate to slow and her breath to steady before she reached down and opened the door to the firm's lobby. She was half surprised that an office this high-end didn't have a buzzer system, but then again, this was Montana.

The lobby was reminiscent of a doctor's office,

complete with the obligatory white orchid in the corner and a water cooler by the door to the main offices. Behind a pane of glass was the secretary's desk, which was conspicuously vacant. The phone was ringing, and she could hear another from somewhere behind the wall of glass.

The hairs on her arms prickled. Something about the place—perhaps it was the eerie quiet on what should have been a busy day, or the fact that she had been on edge since seeing the truck outside, but something didn't feel right.

She sucked in a breath and made her way over to the secretary's area. Certainly, there had to be someone working. Maybe they had just stepped out for a drink or were running an errand for one of the attorneys. Just because her gut was roiling didn't mean anything. Kendra had been on high alert for two days now. If anything, she just needed to get through this meeting, get things handled for her family and hit the bricks.

Approaching the window, she caught a strange scent. At first, she couldn't quite put her finger on it thanks to the thick and heavy aroma of industrial cleaners they must have used in the office, but as she stopped at the marble ledge in front of the secretary's window, she recognized the smell—it was the acrid, metallic scent of gunpowder.

Her hand instinctively moved to her purse, and she wrapped her fingers around her Glock's grip.

This is wrong.

Something's happened here. Something bad.

She did a quick scan around the secretary's desk. At first appearance, she was alone. No signs of a struggle, and nothing was amiss. She didn't dare let her guard down, but she moved closer to the glass after checking the area for potential threats.

The secretary's tan leather chair was pulled out and pointing toward the back offices. On the seat was a long smear of blood. On the floor leading away from it was a series of droplets, as though whoever this blood belonged to had stood up and run, dripping, toward the back.

She moved closer to the glass, hoping to see where the person had gone. As she did, she spotted the bottom of a high-heeled shoe and a woman's ankle; the rest of the woman was out of sight behind a tall desk-like partition. The woman wasn't moving. Perhaps the woman had hit her head…had a bloody nose and passed out on the way to the bathroom.

Any number of things could have happened. This woman can't be dead.

For a moment, she dissociated and found herself wondering why she didn't also smell blood if what she was fearing was true—if the woman was dead, if she had been shot, there would be more blood. Right?

Was this some ploy the office had set up to put her off her game? Was the woman going to jump up like this was all some kind of sick joke?

The phone rang again, pulling her from her disjointed and nonsensical thoughts.

She knocked on the window. "Hello? Are you all right?" The question sounded stupid as she said it aloud. "Ma'am? Are you okay?" she asked again, her voice getting a bit higher with every passing syllable.

She grabbed the door leading to the back and was surprised to find it unlocked. It was heavy, and she opened it just far enough to slip through. It eased closed behind her, and its sluggishness made her wonder if it was the door or if time had slowed down. It could have been her mind's reaction to trauma—that moment in a fight for life or death in which a person's perception heightened and the imperceptible became a still-life reality.

Kendra moved behind the desk. A pool of blood snaked around and slipped under the edges like it was trying to escape. Moving toward the blood, she found the woman. Her face, or what would have been her face, was misshapen and oddly lopsided. The tilt of her head was like she was confused, as if the last thing she'd seen was so out of place that she cocked her head even in death.

The woman appeared to be in her late twenties, and she was looking straight ahead, her eyes dark and sightless as she stared into death's maw. Her hair was curled, and part of it had slipped down and rested in her open mouth. It wasn't until Kendra blinked and focused on the sight in front of her that she realized what was wrong with the woman's face—part of her head was missing where it was pressed into the gray industrial carpet.

Her phone pinged, and a woman's voice sounded from the device. "Nine-one-one, this is Erin. How can we be of assistance?"

In her many years working as a prosecutor, she'd heard many of these kinds of calls on recordings when they played them for judges and juries. Never had she assumed she would be the one who dialed the number—and strangely, she couldn't remember when she had even taken her phone out of her purse.

"Hello?" the dispatcher repeated. "How can I be of assistance?" she repeated, this time her tone taking on a slightly higher sound as though she could sense the fear in Kendra.

It wasn't the first time Kendra had been this close to a dead body, and as she stared at the dark blood, she picked out the little bits of lighter, fatty pink bits that she recognized as pieces of brain. Once, in a case like this, one in which her key witness had been present at the murder, the woman had described how she had screamed. In that case, she said the sound had come from deep in her lungs and from a place so dark within her that she hadn't even recognized that she was the one who had been making the sound.

She stared at the woman's fingernails. Acrylics. Bright pink with jewels and fresh glitter. No nail beds were exposed. She probably had just gotten them done.

"Do you need assistance?" the dispatcher asked, this time really pulling Kendra from her trauma-induced trance.

"Uh," she said, lifting the phone to her ear and falling back into attorney mode—unflappable in the face of the terrifying and unexpected. "Hello, my name is Kendra Spade, and I have just come upon a deceased woman."

She rattled off the building's address. Her voice was even and her affect was flat. If she was on the stand and sounded like this, no one would believe her because of her lack of emotion—especially in a situation in which she was standing in view of a murdered woman.

"Have you taken the woman's pulse?" the dispatcher asked.

She thought about telling the dispatcher that this woman couldn't possibly have a pulse, but instead she found herself on her knees. She pushed back a bit of the woman's dark hair, pulling it out of her mouth and gently moving it over her shoulder, and then pressed her fingers into the still-warm flesh of the woman's neck. "There's no pulse."

"Okay," the dispatcher said. "I have the emergency crews en route to your location. Stay on the phone with me."

She didn't want to stay on the phone. She didn't

want to do anything but get to her feet and leave the office and head straight to the airport and catch the first plane to any place but here. Instead, she did as the dispatcher said. Getting up, she moved down the hallway, where she heard the continuing distinct ring of a cell phone coming from the corner office.

Her stomach clenched as she neared the ringing sound. No attorney she knew would ever let their phone ring for so long without answering it. She tried to convince herself it was nothing, that it was probably just some burner that was left behind and she wouldn't find another scene like that in the lobby. Yet her past and all the horrors she had experienced had her girding her loins. This was one of those times in her life she could pick apart later, but for now she needed to keep being strong and face the reality as it presented itself—gore and all.

The dispatcher was speaking to her, asking her something, but her voice was muffled and drowned out by the fear ringing in Kendra's ears. She held her phone, but her hands drooped to her sides as she nearly floated down the hall.

The office door was open, and she stepped inside. Hanging over the desk was a man. The tips of his brown loafers were grazing the papers on his desk. He was wearing dark blue dress pants and a white button-down shirt with a red satin tie. The brown nylon-looking rope was looped around his neck, his flesh bulging out slightly above the ligature. His skin was bruised and mottled, and his eyes were open and bloodshot—she recognized it as petechia, the breakage of the capillaries in the eye that was indicative of a strangling.

Did this attorney kill the secretary and then hang himself?

Her mind worked fast as she tried to make sense of the scene in front of her. There was no gun on the desk, but some of the man's papers had been pushed off and were scattered haphazardly across the floor. His computer was askew, leaning precariously over the edge, but it was close to his feet. Perhaps he had kicked it and the papers in his attempt to commit suicide? Or was this a murder as well?

Had the secretary seen something threatening— the murderer? Gotten up to run to the attorney's office? Or maybe to lock the door, but she was shot before she had time to stop the assailant? But why would a murderer shoot her and then hang the attorney?

It didn't make sense.

And then she heard it, a strange keening wail. It was almost quiet at first, and then she dropped to her knees and her phone slipped from her hand to the ground. A feeling of sickness filled her. The sound echoing around the office...was coming from her.

A hand touched her shoulder, and the keen turned to the piercing sound of fear as she jerked away from the touch. Standing behind her was the man from the plane. Without even thinking, she pulled out her gun and pointed it up at his center mass. She stared at his face, looking to see if he meant help or harm, but in his eyes she found only questions.

Chapter Four

Trent hadn't meant to scare his mark. He hadn't even been trying to expose that he had been tracking and following her, but this wasn't a normal situation. Nothing about this bounty hunt had been what he considered average—not by a long way, but here they were.

"It's okay," he said, trying to console the woman and get her to calm down. "I'm not here to hurt you. I heard your screams. Are you hurt?" He glanced down to the phone on the ground beside her.

Her gun barrel didn't waver as she closed her mouth and stared at him. Her eyes were wide with fear, and he put his hands up in surrender. "Put the gun down. I'm not here to hurt you."

The barrel dipped slightly. "You're the man from the plane."

He nodded, but he could feel a faint heat rising in his cheeks. This was the first time he'd been made ahead of schedule, and he felt utterly exposed and at a loss. "Yes, but you don't need to worry. I'm not a threat." He reached down and picked up her phone, clicking it off when he saw 911 was still on the other end of the line.

The dispatcher didn't need any more information—they'd be here soon.

"If you're not a threat, then what in the hell are you doing taking my phone away?" She jabbed the gun at him like it was a knife, giving away her fear.

"You put the gun away and I'll give you your phone."

She slipped the gun back into her cross-body purse. "Phone, please."

"Here," he said, handing it back to her. "Is there anyone else here?" He glanced back out into the hallway. There hadn't been time to clear the rooms once he'd rushed in at the sound of her screams, and he was annoyed with his safety oversight, but it was what it was. At the very least, he had made it to her side without taking a bullet. He'd have to chalk that up as a win—even if everything else had gone a bit assways.

"I didn't hear anyone." Kendra looked around like she almost expected someone else to be standing in the corner of the room.

"I'll be right back. You stay here," he said, holding his hand up. "But you sure you're okay? I know this kind of thing can be a shock."

She furrowed her brow. "How would you know? Are you in law enforcement or something?"

Yeah, he wasn't about to answer that line of questions, at least not yet. "We can talk later. I just want to make sure that the killer, if there is one, isn't still here." He slipped out of the room before she could continue her interrogation.

He shouldn't have come in here, but he couldn't bear hearing her screams and doing nothing. She sounded terrified, just as he would have been if he had walked into a situation like this.

From what he'd seen of her, she wasn't the type to frighten easily or to back down. That made her shouts of horror all the more disturbing. He'd found himself wanting to keep her safe, to pull her out of that fear and get her back to her normal state of no-nonsense confidence.

He owed her nothing, no protections; if anything, he had been using her as a means to his end, trying to get to the senator who was suing her family and leaving his holding the bag for a huge bond.

Ever since he'd sat next to her on the plane and then watched her place last night, though, he'd felt an attraction—or at least a curiosity—growing. He wanted to know more about her.

It hadn't been his first stakeout and it wouldn't be his last, but he'd found himself thinking, often with a smile, of how she'd returned fire when her brother lit into her. He liked a woman who could stand her ground.

Yeah, that was it… Her reaction, her scream…

It wasn't the woman he had come to know through his research and short time watching her. She had shown no signs of weakness, not a single one, and yet he had found her huddled on the floor after having fallen to her knees, vulnerable and afraid. That would have made the most hard-hearted man buckle.

As he moved down the hall, he carefully cleared the closest office. It was unoccupied and looked almost identical to the lawyer's office where the man was hanging; books filled the shelves around the desk and there was a series of diplomas adorning the walls. The place was simple, almost austere. He wondered if Kendra's office looked the same in New York City, or if she had pictures of family, something with a sunset, some little article that whispered of the light he sensed in her.

Gah. He was being far too sentimental. It was this scene, the dead bodies, the heightened tensions. Adrenaline spikes could mess with his head.

He focused on the here and now, making sure no threats were still in play.

As soon as they stepped out of this office, there was a high probability that they would give their statements to the police and then never see each other again. There wasn't a damned reason she would want to keep him around, especially after she found out what he had really been up to.

If she had done her research, she had probably already run across documents that could tie him to the senator, this office and, *hell*…probably even the dead bodies.

She hadn't seemed to recognize him as anything other than her seatmate on the airline, but she'd had no real reason to dig into the bond Dean Clark had received, which had allowed him to leave the jail while he was awaiting his trial. She was only here for a civil lawsuit, not for his criminal proceedings.

Maybe, though, it was potentially advantageous to her for him to get his hands on the senator as well.

Yeah, that's it… Make it about her.

That had worked with his ex whenever he had found himself in trouble. Given, the fix was only a Band-Aid as there were a medley of other issues between them.

He cleared the next office and the next. The floor was empty aside from them and the two deceased officemates.

When he came back to Kendra, he found her standing and looking over something in her cell phone. Her clothing and hair were perfectly in place, and her face had taken on the stony look that he had noticed her wearing the first time they had unofficially met.

"Clear?" she asked, clipped.

He nodded.

"So, are you going to tell me who you are before the police arrive?" She gave him the side-eye as she barely glanced up from her phone.

The simple look made him tense. Even when she was pressing for answers he didn't want to give, she was sexy...though intimidating.

He couldn't remember the last time anyone had intimidated him.

Yeah, he was definitely playing ball out of his league with this woman.

"Name's Trent."

"Trent." She said it like it had a bitter aftertaste. "And what were you doing here, Trent?"

"I could ask the same of you," he countered, but he was careful to keep his tone neutral and nonescalating. He wasn't trying to start a fight, only trying to take her sights off him.

"I was here for a meeting with..." She glanced up at the face of the man who was hanging from the bar between two ceiling tiles. "Well, I was here for a meeting with someone I assume was him."

Trent looked at the nameplate on the office's door. It read,

Brad Bradshaw, Esq.
Attorney-at-Law

He nearly chuckled. What parent would stick their kid with a name like that? It made him think of the old country song "A Boy Named Sue."

Maybe Brad's parents wanted him to grow up and be some overstuffed fraternity boy. If so, they had nailed it. Though he instantly felt bad for even thinking such a thing about the dead. He didn't know the man personally. He couldn't pass any sort of judgment against him. If anything, someone already had, and if he thought about the man now, it didn't really matter.

There were the sounds of police sirens and the screeching of tires on hot asphalt as the first responders arrived. More than likely, he'd know a few of the boys who were going to pound up the stairs leading to this place.

He looked out the window, careful not to disturb anything his potential friends would need to piece together the scene and make their case.

"What are you doing?" Kendra asked.

"Looks like you're going to be all right. I'll go catch up with the police. Let them know I've cleared the scene." He knew it wouldn't matter what in the hell he said to them, but he wasn't ready for them to completely blow his cover. Maybe he could still turn this entire situation—and his poor attempt to help Kendra—into something he could work with and keep both of them satisfied.

He moved out of the office and toward the lobby, but as he did, the first of the officers bounded in. "Hello? This is Officer Jared Dell of the Missoula City Police Department. Is anyone here?"

He cleared his throat as he walked out into the waiting area of the lobby with his hands in clear view. "Heya, Jared. How's it going?"

"Trent? What in the hell are you doing here?" Jared asked as his hand moved nearly imperceptibly away from his weapon.

At least he had saved himself from having two guns pointed at him within the hour.

"Looks like there are a couple of people down in the back."

"What about the woman who made the call? Is she still here?" Jared asked, looking around Trent and glancing at the door leading to the offices.

"Yeah, she's down in the last office at the end of the hall. There's a guy hanging back there."

"She have anything to do with these deaths, as far as you know?"

Trent shook his head. "I don't think so. I saw her walk in right ahead of me. She didn't have time."

Jared nodded and his hand moved away from his utility belt. Some of the immediacy seemed to seep from the officer's mannerisms.

"Anyone else you saw?" Jared asked.

He shook his head.

"Good, then I'm gonna ask for you to wait outside for me, and then I'm going to need to ask you some more questions."

Trent sighed. "Actually, I was hoping I could run back to the shop for a bit. If you need me, you know where I'll be. Cool?"

He was aware it wasn't protocol to have a potential witness leave without making a statement, but he also knew they were going to be here for the next few hours poring over the scene and the bodies.

"You see anything, anything at all?" Jared asked.

"Nope. Just found the woman who called it in on her knees screaming from the back office. Cleared the place. Then you showed up." He shrugged.

The door to the waiting room opened, and Jared's hand instinctively moved to his gun as Kendra walked out. She ran her hand over her hair. "If you don't mind, I would like to go with this man as well. I could use some air."

Jared shot Trent a look, like he suddenly was trying to figure out exactly who this woman was to him and why she would press for the same kind of good-ol'-boy treatment he had been requesting.

"I'd like you to stay, if you don't mind. Just for a few questions." Jared looked back at Kendra.

Trent stepped forward. He knew she needed a breather, even if she put on a strong face. "It's okay. She's with me. We're both available, not going anywhere. You know how to reach me."

Jared looked from one to the other. "Well, I suppose it would be all right. I have your contact information, and I will let the detective know. But you need to stay together, understood?"

Trent slipped her a sideways glance, and she gave him a tip of the head. "Looks like you have a deal."

They brushed by three more officers as they made their way down the stairs and out to the parking lot.

It was full of cruisers, and the ambulance that was just pulling up to the building was forced to park on the road. Her ranch truck was boxed in, but he didn't say anything. Not only would they be spending what was likely the rest of the day together, she was also going to have to ride around with him—that was until she lost it on him and got a taxi.

This was going to be one hell of a day. It already was one.

"Are we both going to pretend like you aren't going to have to be my chauffeur?" she asked, a smile on her face.

"I didn't want…" He paused, not quite sure what to say that wouldn't make him look foolish.

"We promised the good deputy that we would stick together until we chatted with the detectives. I'm a woman of my word. And you know as well as I do that my truck isn't going anywhere." She shrugged. "Can't say I'm too upset about it. I'm not much one for driving."

It came as a bit of a surprise that she, this woman who so clearly loved to be in control, would be willing to give up the keys and be shuttled around. Maybe he had misjudged her.

"Besides, I need to catch up on a little work." She lifted her phone.

"No rest for the weary," he said, giving her a slight nod as he motioned toward his pickup.

"Your friend back there seemed to know exactly

who you were and where we are going. I'd be happy to be brought up to speed." She sent him a warm smile that he was sure had opened many a door.

If he told her the truth now, there would be no going back. Everything would hinge on her being able to accept him and his motives. If she didn't, game over.

He walked to his pickup and opened the passenger side door for her, but instead of getting in, she merely looked at him and waited for his answer.

Here goes nothing.

"I work over at Lockwood Bonds. I'm a bondsman and the occasional bounty hunter," he said, fearing to embellish or expound. He was who he was, and what would come would come.

"Oh?" She cocked her head as she stared at him, their eyes locking. "And what did you say your last name was, Trent?"

This woman was damned smart and definitely someone he was not going to outmaneuver. "Lockwood, ma'am."

"I see." She put her hand on the top of the hood and tapped her nails on its surface with a *clickety-click-thump* sound.

Everything he had seen about this woman had the power to bring her enemies and her friends to their knees.

Without another word, she got in and buckled up. He closed the door behind her and then let out a long sigh as he strode to the driver's side. Even in his relief, he couldn't help the nagging feeling that he very well could have been heading to the firing squad.

They were quiet as he got in and made his way onto the main road. He was going to have a hard time trying to explain his sudden appearance in the shop, his former mark's bait in tow, to his brother.

"You hungry? Want to get some food before we have to be on lockdown at the shop? I'm sure the detective won't come to see us until this evening at the earliest. This kind of thing, in a small town, tends to take up a lot of time and bandwidth for the police department."

She was looking down at her phone, and he ventured a glance at what she was doing. From what he could tell before she tipped the screen away from him, she was sending emails.

"So, you're from New York?" he asked.

"You know the answer to that. You've been following me for the last few days." She didn't say it like it was a question or an accusation, just a simple observance.

He swallowed back the guilt rising in his throat. There was no way she could have noticed him outside her cabin or at the ranch.

Which made him wonder...if she had known he was following her, how had she not known who he was? Was this just her attempt to fish information out of him and get him to admit something she had no proof of?

"Myself, I'm not much of a New York man. Though your food is something." He sent her a smile, but instead of disarming her, he could sense her tightening up.

"If you don't mind, I'm not one who particularly enjoys small talk. Especially when there are larger issues at hand," she countered, her voice smooth and practiced.

"You're a tough cookie, you know that?" He tried to avoid the jab of her words.

She chuckled lightly as she tapped on her phone. "Not the first time I've heard that one, but thank you for the compliment."

He hadn't meant it as a compliment or a criticism, just as a statement. She was who she was, but damned if he didn't find her confidence and no-nonsense attitude intriguing.

She hadn't answered him about lunch, so instead of asking again, he turned and headed toward his favorite haunt—a little dive bar with cheap beer and prime rib available all day. If he was going to have to do this dance, he was at least going to get his favorite meal in his belly.

The Wolf Lodge was a dive bar in every sense of the word. It had been around longer than he'd been alive. The building listed like most of its patrons upon their leaving. In college, he'd spent more than a few nights in this place with his buddies and his brother. Most of his friends had moved and a couple had passed away—one to a car accident and another to cancer. The thought made him feel old, even though he was only in his early thirties.

It was tough, losing the ones in his life who'd been a part of his growing up. Justin, the friend who'd died in a car accident, had always wanted to be a cop. He would have loved seeing where Trent had gone with his life, and especially all the guns he got to train with and handle.

He parked to the left of the log building's entrance. Kendra finally really looked up from her phone and seemed to be trying to make sense of where they were. She moved to open her door but then dropped her hand to the leg of her suit pants and paused. "Hey, do you mind if we run somewhere first? Before we eat?"

"What do you mean?" He frowned at her.

"There is no way I'm walking into a place like that wearing this," she said, motioning at her bloody clothes. "You know as well as I do that I would stick out even without the blood. Gossip would pick up, and any anonymity I was hoping for would disappear. I'm sure that my family wants me to fly below the radar given what they do."

"I can run you home, if you like." He was careful to avoid the subject of the ranch.

She shook her head. "No, the last thing I want is to go back there."

It was strange, the feeling in his gut when she finally opened up to him. Her admission and little bit of insight made the ambiguity and guilt build within him, but at the very least she must have bought his little white lie—or rather, his avoidance of the truth.

"Where do you need me to take you? There's a mall near the center of town. It doesn't have much by way of high-end brands, but you might find something to your taste."

She chuckled, and the sound made some of his nerves dissipate. Maybe they could be friends after all.

"Why don't you run me to the ranch supply store? They have clothes, right?" She tapped on her phone.

"Yeah, but the fact you are using your phone to look up what they have kind of goes against the spirit of the place," he teased.

"Oh?" She gave him the raise of a brow. "Why would you say that? People don't use the internet here?"

He gave a full, real laugh at the absurdity.

When she smiled, for a split second, he forgot about the horrors that had brought them together and to this moment. She was breathtaking when her face lit up; it was like he could feel the warmth radiate from her when she was happy. Or maybe he had been in the dark so long that being around this woman just did that to him.

Now that she seemed to have recovered her equilibrium, he was losing his. They were two strangers bound together by a horrible tragedy. He wished all they'd just witnessed could go away. He yearned for their respective cases to disappear, too. He wanted to just drive off with her by his side and start the day over—his *life* over. Would she want the same thing?

He shook that thought from his mind.

It wasn't far to the store, where the parking lot was full of ranch trucks, Subarus, prebuilt chicken coops and water troughs for livestock. As they walked inside, they were met with the familiar scent of industrial cleaners, wood chips and horse feed. He'd always loved that aroma; it was a heady mix of everything that was Montana.

As she walked in, he glanced over at her to see if she took in the scent in the same way or if she cringed and wrinkled her nose at the not entirely pleasant odor. Instead, she tilted her head back and closed her eyes, unintentionally inhaling the place as naturally as he had. She really was full of endearing surprises.

"The women's section is over here," he said, motioning to the left.

"Are there chicks here, too?" she asked, an edge of childlike excitement suddenly in her voice.

"It's a little late in the year, but we can walk back

and take a peek if you like," he said with a smile. He nearly extended his hand so he could lead her, but he resisted the urge and instead motioned toward the right.

"You've spent a lot of hours in here, I see." She smiled like there was something about the idea she liked.

"Yeah, I grew up on a cattle ranch just east of here in Hall. Ranch supply stores were my mall as a kid."

"Hall?"

"Little town, a coach stop near Drummond. Don't feel bad that you haven't heard of it. Most people haven't."

As they neared the area with live animals, the smell of wood chips intensified. On his left, he spotted large areas glassed in for bunnies.

"So, you are a real-life cowboy who became a bondsman?"

"Odd life path, ya know," he said, though he was sure hers was nothing like his own. She was probably the kind of woman who grew up knowing whom she wanted to be and what she wanted to accomplish with her life and then followed the straightest and most efficient Ivy League path to get there.

"I know a thing or two about those. I've always found as soon as I think I have the right answers, something else comes up—both professionally and privately."

The way her shoulders rose as she spoke made

him wonder exactly what had happened in her private life that had made her instinctively move to protect herself. As she seemed to be opening up to him naturally, he didn't push it and instead pocketed the question for another time. For now, all he wanted was for her to feel free to be herself—unjudged and unchecked by him.

Watching her move toward the women's section, he was further reminded how she could change her clothes and she could love what he loved, but she would never really fit in here. All they could ever be was two strangers with a shared target.

Chapter Five

Though she was aware she was only putting off dealing with what she had seen at the Bradshaw offices by agreeing to stay with Trent, Kendra couldn't help but admit she liked the man—liked how he'd given her room and respect. For a brief moment, he had been the oasis in the desert, giving her a respite from the ravages of her life and the reality in which they found themselves.

AJ popped up in her text messages again. Of course, she'd had to let him know what had happened, and of course he wasn't happy about it. He'd even gone so far as to ask her if she'd had anything to do with the deaths in veiled language—but not veiled enough if it were used in a court of law. But she wasn't like the rest of the family—immune, by and large, to death.

If she clicked on his text message, it wouldn't change what had occurred, and right now she had just as many questions as AJ likely did and even fewer answers. He could wait. She wasn't one of his employees he could boss around.

Another text popped up from him.

How did her brothers and sister put up with his constant hounding? They all seemed to get along pretty well, which meant that it was likely only her that had a problem with his authority—or lack thereof. One more reason to hang out with Trent now—so she wouldn't have to face her family after this morning's fiasco.

Maybe AJ was just harder to deal with because he was aware he held no real power over her. Regardless, she needed to catch her breath for a moment before she could give him the attention that he clearly so desperately required.

"You look like you got bad news," Trent said as she got into his car wearing her brand-new clothes and a brown leather pair of Justin boots.

"That easy to tell? I always thought I had a pretty good poker face," she said, covering the truth of her words with a dismissive chuckle.

"I just happen to know the face of disappointment fairly well, given my line of work." He started the car and they hit the road.

She wasn't sure if they were going back to get food or not, but she was hoping for something and so was her stomach, which was rumbling so loudly she wondered if Trent could actually hear it.

"I'm familiar with bounties, obviously, but I can't say I've ever actually met a bounty hunter. What is it that you do…you know, when you are hunting for people who owe your company money?"

He seemed to jerk slightly at her question, and there was something about his reaction that made her suspicions rise. She had tested him before, feeling him out to see if he had been tracking her, but he'd seemed innocent. Had she been wrong?

"Hunting may mean a different thing here than it does in the city. Here it means you are hell-bent on killing something. I'm a lot of things, but a killer isn't one of them."

"I didn't mean any offense, really. My apologies," she said, reaching over and gently placing her fingers on his arm. His arm was thick with muscles, and they flexed under her fingers, feeling like stone. *Damn, he is hot.*

"Don't worry, it takes a lot more than asking about my job to offend me." He sent her a gentle smile, absolving her of any guilt. "As far as my methods, I don't know about in New York, but here we are law enforcement officers and granted the same privileges—with a lot less oversight."

"Did you want to be a police officer?" As she asked the question, she realized he might take it as an admonishment of his profession, as though it was less than, but she was hopeful he would see her intention for what it was—curiosity.

He shook his head. "Nah. If I could start my life all over again, I think I'd be a country music singer. I always thought I sounded a little like Chris LeDoux."

He hummed a chorus she vaguely recognized, but she couldn't say she was familiar with country music. For the first time, she wished she was.

She hated this feeling of constantly being a square peg in a round hole and not really fitting in anywhere she went. Try as she might to chameleon her way through every situation, there were times that no amount of changing her clothes could make her quite fit. She picked off a piece of lint that had come from her new blue jeans.

"You look good...*real* good, actually. You don't have a thing to feel uncomfortable about."

There he went reading her again. He definitely was a member of the law enforcement brethren. It raised the question of how rigidly he adhered to the stereotype. From what she had seen of him so far, he seemed like he colored outside the lines and was comfortable with it—but the same could be said of many agents, operatives and officers.

"Do you always do that?" she asked, smiling.

"What is *that*, exactly?"

"Trying to make grown women blush," she teased, trying to take the attention off her visible discomfort.

"Ha! Do you think that's what I'm up to?" He lifted a brow. "I can't say that I think myself capable of making you blush. I bet you've been around better-looking men than me, a cowboy breathing down middle age's neck."

She stared at the little lines that were starting at the corners of his brown eyes. He glanced over at her, catching her gazing at him. He threw his head back in one of the sexiest laughs she had ever just seen. "You see it, don't you?"

She wanted to tell him "not at all," which was absolutely the truth. He was incredibly handsome, but she kept her mouth closed. If she said something like that, she was experienced enough to know it would send them down an ill-advised path of flirting, which would lead to thinking about kissing, then really kissing and then all the things that came after kissing and ended with her getting back on a plane and wishing she hadn't compromised her emotions. As much as she was attracted to the man beside her, and was growing to like him, she loved herself more. This time her need for self-protection outweighed the needs of her belly. She was wound up tight after the morning's tragedy, and she knew herself well enough to realize it was better to tamp down the high energy coursing through her now instead of letting it run in the wrong direction.

"All I see is a man who is working to do his job to the best of his abilities."

His smile disappeared, and she was reminded that once again she was saying all the wrong things if she wanted to keep this man as just a friend.

The last man who had hit on her had been on the other side of a conference table during a plea deal negotiation. He was the defendant and on trial for first-degree murder after shooting two people in a twenty-four-hour convenience store.

Maybe that was why she was a little jaded when it came to accepting compliments or come-ons, even gentle ones.

It seemed more than possible that her job had set her up for a lifetime of failed relationships. When she had found herself in one, what few there were, she had a way of picking men who needed her to save them—one from his mother and the next from whiskey. She was great at her job, but when it came to being a crutch for needy men, she was less than capable. For once, she would have liked to be with a man who could bring as much determination and intelligence to the table as she did, or at least one who could stand on his own two feet and not only take care of himself but perhaps protect her as well.

"I'm glad you think I'm doing a good job," Trent said, an apologetic look in his eyes as he glanced at her.

"Were you following me from New York? Tracking me?" she countered.

He didn't meet her gaze. It was fine; he didn't have to say anything his body hadn't already—even if she had avoided acknowledging it fully right up until this moment.

She should have followed her gut from the very first moment she had seen this man. Intuition—especially hers, which had been shaped by years of manipulations in the courtroom—was something she relied on, and yet she had tried to ignore it, to this man's benefit. Why? Why had she allowed her emotions to come into play when she should have been running purely on logic and the information that had been presented to her?

This was what happened when she attempted to trust another human being—and not just another human, but a man. Men always let her down. She pressed her fingers to the puckered bullet scar beneath her clavicle. The last time she had trusted a man, he had pulled the trigger and it had nearly cost her life.

Single, all she depended on was herself, and there was less of a chance of being disappointed or hurt. Plus, she was happy enough alone. She liked her private time, her space and her routines.

She needed to focus on the job at hand—protecting her family. They were more important than anything, and should the senator continue his lawsuit—which no doubt he would, albeit with a new counselor—she was the only one with the power to stop him in his legal tracks.

"It wasn't personal." He finally broke the silence.

She simply nodded. They were at an impasse— the best way she could handle the lawsuit was to get the senator alone and convince him it was against his best interest to pursue any further legal action…but that kind of persuading often required a strong arm, one she was certain Trent could provide.

"What is in it for you if you get your hands on the senator?" she asked.

"He owes my family a lot of money—the bond and

interest. The kind of money where, if he doesn't return it, it's gonna run our business into the ground." He ran his hand over his face, making her wonder about everything he wasn't telling her.

She filed away the info he'd given her. A bail jumper wasn't exactly an upstanding citizen, and that could help her family in the suit.

"How long you guys been in business?" she asked.

"About five years. Before that it was my dad's business." There was a strain in his voice that told her of family secrets.

Regardless of what those secrets were, he definitely had skin in this game and just as much to lose as she and her family did. For her family, however, it wasn't just about the money—it was also their reputation at stake. They already had a black eye professionally thanks to the senator's family. If they lost the lawsuit, their business was as good as gone. And, no doubt, she would be the family's whipping girl.

"Why do you think someone would want Bradshaw dead?" Kendra asked.

"I hate to say it…" he started, pulling into the lot and parking the car in front of the restaurant. "But the only people I know who could have anything to really gain from his death are you and your family."

Chapter Six

Aside from ordering their lunch, Trent and Kendra had barely spoken. She had been careful to avoid eye contact with him, like she was thinking about all the reasons she hated him and the comment he had made about her family having reason to kill… even if he had a point.

If that wasn't enough, the two-bit bar was clearly so far outside her comfort zone that it might as well have been on Mars. If they were going to have a real conversation, though, maybe making her uncomfortable was to his advantage. She seemed like the kind of woman who commanded every room she entered, but if he was going to get any real answers from her and they were actually going to work together, the only way forward was to know where they both stood—which meant complete honesty.

Kendra was staring off in the direction of the elk shoulder mount hanging over the bar. The massive bull was staring off in the ethereal distance, just like the woman looking in his direction.

"I don't think my brothers would've sent me to that meeting if they had anything to do with that murder." Kendra finally looked back at him, and it surprised him that she must have been thinking about his opinion for this long. In fact, he would've guessed she was looking for an escape rather than for answers.

"But you see where I was coming from, that your family are the ones that have the most to gain by taking out the senator's legal team."

Kendra nodded. "Oh, definitely. But as much as my family and I butt heads, they wouldn't have sent me in there to be the one to discover the murders if they had been behind them. They are pretty protective." She sighed. "That is to say, if this wasn't just a simple murder-suicide. Who the hell knows—maybe the attorney had a breaking point with his secretary? Maybe they were having an affair and there had been a fight. Any number of scenarios could've played out back at that office."

She was grasping for straws, anything that had him looking in another direction than her family. Yet he wasn't the one she needed to worry about. Though he worked with law enforcement, he didn't need to seek justice. Not in the same way as an officer. If anything, if it came out that she or her family was involved, he would have to make damned sure to distance himself from the mess and the eventual fallout.

"I hope your family didn't have anything to do

with this. If they did, we're both going to be in more trouble than even we can handle."

"I'm aware—my career hangs on them not screwing me over." She waved at the bartender and motioned for a Bud Light. The man gave her a stiff nod. "What makes you think they'd do something like that? Did someone say something?"

"No—" he shook his head "—I just have found that sometimes it is the ones right under our noses who wish us the most harm." She shifted uncomfortably in her chair, making him wish he hadn't said anything. "Have you always lived in New York?"

She shook her head. "I used to have a more… *active role* in the family business." Her fingers fluttered over a spot near her neck. The bartender walked over and set a bottle of Bud Light in front of her, but he stood there for just a second too long. She frowned and looked up at him. "Thanks, you can put it on our tab."

The man stared at her for a second longer, and his gaze drifted down to her chest before he seemed to comprehend her words. "You got it, doll. Don't be afraid to let me know if y'all need anything else."

She cringed as the man called her *doll*.

Sensing her discomfort, he glared at the bartender. "Hey, man, thanks for the drink, but you need to keep your eyes to yourself," Trent said, waving the guy away.

A faint blush rose in her cheeks as the burly bartender spun around and grumbled something under his breath.

"Sorry about that. I don't think the men around here are used to…well, *women like you*." He cringed at the way his words sounded, but they were the best he could come up with on the spot.

Great, now we're both uncomfortable.

She let out a small laugh, catching him even more off guard. "That's not it. Thank you for…well… Was that a compliment—'women like me'?"

Now he was the one blushing. "You know it was."

She chuckled as she took a sip of the beer and set it back down. "I just… It's been a long time since anybody's called me anything other than a cold-hearted…woman."

He found that hard to believe. "You and me both, sister. Though I guess I've never been called a woman. Way I see it, would be a compliment if I was. Women are a hell of a lot tougher and more re-silient than men."

She threw her head back as she laughed. "Now I know you're just trying to get on my good side." She took a long drink of beer, smiling as she did.

"Come now, why would you say that?" It was nice seeing her start to finally relax around him and moving past some of the events of the day and his idiocy.

"You have to know that I'm all about strong women. And you're just using that to get in my good graces. Regardless, well played, sir." She tipped the beer bottle in his direction in respect.

He could've guessed. He liked that about her. "I do like strong-willed women. My mother was one. My grandmother, her mother, was called the battle-ax, but obviously not by me—I wasn't that stupid." He laughed, recalling his German grandmother whose footfalls were as commanding as her presence. There had been nothing delicate about the woman, especially when she started yelling at his grandfather in their native tongue.

"If she was anything like the women in my family, if you had called her anything other than *ma'am*, you wouldn't be sitting here with me now." Kendra sent him an endearing smile. "I don't understand why some men and women need to condemn any female who can conduct herself well in a fight. Not all women were put on this earth to be dependent on others for their own emotional or physical well-being."

He nodded. "None of the women in my life could be called codependent. If anything, for all the ups and downs, our matriarchs were the ones who kept our family from falling apart. My grandmother's the reason my brother and I run the business together like we do." He felt them edging toward a conversation he wasn't sure he was ready to have about how little he and his brother saw eye to eye. Even though he had wanted to have open communication with

Kendra, it was far easier when the pressure was on her to tell him her secrets rather than him exposing his own. Maybe it was the drama of the morning that had him opening up. Or maybe it was just her. "But what about your family? You used to work with them?"

She grew rigid. "I used to be a contractor, but I lost my taste for it after I took a round that I should have known was coming. I'll never go back." She touched that spot below her clavicle and then took a sip of her beer. "I prefer standing in a courtroom. So here I am, once again working for my family even though I promised myself I would never be back in the fold."

He could see she knew how to handle herself; when she'd had her gun on him, that had been more than obvious. This woman really was unique. She'd had one hell of a life.

"I won't ask what made you get out of the game, but I understand the conditions out there. I looked into going into contracting a few years out of school, and I couldn't have done the work. I have a lot of respect for what your family does, though."

She took a long drink of her beer. "My family is tougher than the rest, that's for sure. While we have all done our duty, none of us are cold-blooded killers. We aren't hit men."

He nodded, though he was surprised she would admit he could have been right about them. "I didn't want to offend you earlier, but if it walks like a duck and talks like a duck…" He shrugged. "That being said, it doesn't make any sense for them to send you into a hornet's nest if they are behind this. That is, unless they wanted to teach you some kind of lesson or pin this thing on you…"

She shook her head violently. "My siblings are huge pains in the ass, and we don't get along all the time, but when push comes to shove, they will always have my back. We were raised to be a cohesive unit, even in adversity. Actually, in adversity more than any other time." There was a look on her face that he couldn't quite read, but if he had to guess, it appeared to be some kind of guilt.

He glanced away from her as the server sauntered over, carrying a tray of food. She lowered it on her arm, and as she did, Trent caught a whiff of the prime rib. It smelled like rosemary and cracked pepper, and it made his mouth water. After the waitress got them settled and disappeared, Kendra finally looked back at him. "Are you okay? You've gotten quiet."

He forced himself to smile, hoping to disarm her. "I'm fine," he said, jabbing his fork into the steak and slicing off a bite. "You try your steak yet?"

"Not yet." She looked down at the slab of meat on her plate. It was one degree away from having hooves and mooing, and he wasn't sure, based on her expression, if she appreciated the rareness or not.

"We can send it back," he offered, looking past

her to where the waitress had gone, but she was nowhere to be seen. Instead, there was a big dude with
a T-shirt with the local railroad workers' union logo
emblazoned on its front standing a few feet behind
Kendra and looking over her shoulder and down her
shirt.

"Hey, man, if you're hungry, you need to order
your own steak. That one is the lady's." He could
feel his lip curl with disgust. Kendra turned around,
glaring at the man.

The dude tore his gaze off Kendra's breasts just
long enough to sneer at him, then he looked back at
her. "You know you can do better," the railroad guy
said with a smirk. "This guy—" he pointed at Trent
"—couldn't punch his way out of a paper bag. You
deserve a guy who can kick some ass." With that, he
placed a dirty paw on her shoulder in a gesture both
possessive and menacing, as if he were daring either
of them to stop his advances. Trent saw her wince
as the man squeezed the spot she'd rubbed earlier.

Kendra slowly turned back to him, pulled her nap-
kin off her lap and set it upon the table. There was a
thin smile on her lips as she looked at Trent. He had
the sense she was up to something, and he shook his
head, but her smile only widened as she stood up.
"What did you say your name was?" she asked, her
voice as smooth as silk as she faced the man.

"Why? You wanna scream it later?" the guy countered.

"No," she said with a laugh. "I just like to know the names of the guys whose asses *I* kick." She closed the gap with the man.

Before Trent even had the chance to make sense of what she was saying, the base of Kendra's hand connected squarely with the man's nose. There was a sickening crunch as it snapped under her palm thrust.

Trent jumped to his feet, and the metal bar chair he'd been sitting on dropped to the ground behind him with a metallic *clunk*. He rushed toward her as the man looked in Kendra's direction, but there was a disconnect between the man's eyes and his movements. The guy looked like he was trying to raise his fist to strike her. Without dropping her elbow or giving away her punch, Kendra struck the guy again.

The man crumpled at her feet in a heap of blood and blubber.

"Holy crap. Kendra. Damn," Trent said, shocked at her quick response. He knew women could be vicious and take a man down, but he'd never seen a woman do it so quickly or effectively in anything but movies.

"Who's screaming now?" she said to the man, her voice soft as molten chocolate but cold as steel. "Touch me again, and I'll really make you howl."

"What in the hell is going on?" The bartender charged out from behind the bar in their direction.

The two other men that had been with the railroad worker started to move toward Trent. The fight was going to be on, and part of him loved the idea. The last time he'd taken somebody down—when he wasn't on the job—was in college.

Kendra reached into her purse and threw some money on the table. She grabbed Trent's hand and pulled him toward the door. "Let's get out of here."

Part of him yearned for the fight, to feel the sting of the punch as he landed a hammer fist. The guy's friends were moving toward him, but the bartender swerved into their path, cutting them off as he made his way toward the door behind Kendra. They were bigger than him, but with a few leg strikes he could even the playing field.

As they made it outside, she strode toward his car, unrushed, as if she knew the toughs inside the bar wouldn't follow. "Keys. I'm driving."

There wasn't a chance in hell he would argue. This woman was one major badass.

Chapter Seven

He reached in his pocket and threw the keys in her direction as she rushed to the driver's side. They piled into the car, and there was a spray of gravel as she charged out of the parking lot.

"You told me you were a contractor, but I guess... Well, I thought I would have to save you."

"It's okay." She reached over and took his hands. "Just take a breath. We are out of there."

"No thanks to me. Holy crap. Seriously..."

She shot him a lopsided smile. "I told you I came from the family business. I just didn't tell you about my Muay Thai days."

"Just when I thought you couldn't get any cooler." The words were out of his mouth and flopping around the car like a dying fish before he had a chance to reel them back.

His eyes widened as he tried to think of a way to cover his misstep. "I mean..." he continued, fumbling his words, "you are just so much more than I thought you'd be when I first saw you."

She cleared her throat and let go of him. Opening and closing her fist, she glanced down at her knuckles. They were starting to swell, and the middle two were turning black and blue.

"I'm rusty." She raised her hand in the air so he could get a better view, but he had no doubt it was also so she could divert the focus from his moronic move of telling her exactly what he thought about her.

"Why do you say that?"

She wiggled her fingers then dropped her hand back to the steering wheel. "If I'd hit him properly, the bruising would be even over all my knuckles instead of just the two. I'm surprised I even made him drop. Only thing I had going for me was the fact I caught him off guard."

He nodded. "It's fair to say you caught us all off our game."

"In my world, and doing what I do, it pays to know how to drop an enemy without them ever even seeing the strike." She smiled. "Now, where's your shop?"

He pointed for her to turn left and head down Broadway toward downtown and the courthouse. "How long have you been doing martial arts?"

She smiled again. "Long enough to know my way around a set of elbows." She glanced over at him. "About the bond. You said you were worried about getting your family's investment back... Wouldn't

there have been some sort of collateral that he offered up, or someone who signed as an indemnitor?"

"Yeah," he said, relieved. Work was a safe subject
to turn to. Though he knew he shouldn't feel inept
in not having come to her rescue, there was still a
twinge of something in his gut—he had wanted to
save her.

She slowed the truck down. "I can tell something
is wrong."

He chuckled, embarrassed that she could so easily read him. "I was just… Well, I should be your
protector. I know it's stupid. You know…a *typical*
guy kind of instinct."

She gave him a soft smile. "Not stupid, and I appreciate your desire to help. Someday, I may need it."
She tapped her fingers on the steering wheel. "The
truth is, I've had to learn to be my own protector. I
don't know any other way to be. I've gone through
so many years of heartache and constant attacks. I've
had to fight for every opinion I have and what is left
of my personal life and my identity."

He hadn't thought about that, but it made sense.
Here was a woman people loved to hate. Even other
attorneys probably hated her and worked to under-
mine her—and maybe they weren't the harshest of
her critics. As a prosecutor, she probably had a lot
of enemies.

"I'm not judging you," he said, suddenly wishing he was anywhere but stuck in this car with her.

He had a feeling anything he said right now would be wrong, and all he really wanted to do was make her happy and get out of this moment somewhat unscathed.

"Yes, you are judging, and that's okay. It's what humans do," she said, an edge to her voice. "You know what really pisses me off, though? It's when someone calls me *too much*." She gripped the wheel tight. "Why is it wrong for a woman to be powerful, to be smart? I shouldn't have to hide that to make people—especially men—more comfortable because they think I'm *too much*."

He could tell where this was going, and he wished he held the answers she needed to hear. "You're not too much for the people who want and need you in their lives."

She chuffed. "No need for flattery. No one wants me unless they can use me. Do you know how tiring that can be? Even now, coming here... I was forced into it. Forced to act for a man who *needed* me."

He nodded, afraid to say anything.

"And here you are—you need me to be on your side...and on your team for this case. But you know what? What if I want to just be on my own personal team, the Kendra team, a one-woman outfit? I just want to get the answers and get back to *my* life."

He reached for the door handle and looked out the window. If he jumped right now and tucked and rolled, they were going slowly enough that he could probably survive the landing.

"Just as an example, I'm sure that I'm intimidating you right now," she said, gesturing at him and his hand clamped around the door handle. "As much as I feel bad about it, why should I?"

"Mmm-hmm," he said, trying to validate her feelings while also not being drawn into her personal problems. He didn't know, nor could he possibly understand, how she was feeling. "I think you are incredible, just as you are. Sure, I bet there are people who are intimidated by you, but why should you care?"

She studied him. "Why do you say that?"

He appreciated that she was coming to him for validation even though she was clearly fighting against herself and struggling with her need for affirmation.

"There will always be people who don't like you, or me. It's just part of being human. There isn't anything wrong with people not liking you—and I think you know that and at a logical level are totally okay with it. Yet I think you are struggling with the emotional toll it is taking on you. You're not alone in your struggle."

"Thanks. What do I owe you for this session?" she joked, then turned serious. "Do you feel the same way—like you are never enough?" She pulled into the parking spot directly in front of the bond shop, parallel parking in a series of jarring motions back and forth.

He laughed. "I just know that no matter what, I'll never please some people. And even though I know that, I still find myself trying to do more—satisfy everyone. But truthfully, what bothers me more is the fact that I'm afraid. I hate being *afraid*."

She put the car in Park and turned toward him. "You don't have to lie to me to try and win favor. I know you're strong. You're tough. You aren't scared of anything. If you were, there's no way you would travel around the country hunting down criminals— and people like me." She scowled at him.

He could feel her question resting in the air.

"To be clear, I wasn't hunting you. Just following you to my objective."

"Semantics." She waved off the conversation, like it was a hornet threatening to sting them both. "About the indemnitor?"

"You mean the bond cosigner?"

She nodded. "Or was there collateral?"

Of course, she would bring it all back to the task at hand. That was easier than the emotional conversation they'd been having. He got that. "Because of the death of Senator Clark's wife, and her not having a will, most of her assets—including their home— were sent to probate. As such, we had to have a co-signer on the bond in that moment, a woman named Marla Thomas."

"And you've looked into her?" Kendra asked.

He nodded. "My brother Tripp was the one who met her when she came in to sign the papers, but he hasn't said much. He should have done his legwork and done a full-blown background on her, but I've not seen it. Now she's pretty much in the wind. I haven't been able to pull a damned thing about her."

"There has to be something," she said.

"I hear you, but I can only do so much. Besides, I'd rather get my hands on the senator—he's the real piece of work. Maybe the woman just wised up about the guy and hit the road."

"Do you think the senator had a relationship with her, one he could leverage? Maybe he could manipulate her into signing for him because he intended on skipping and slapping her with the debt?" She turned off the engine and put the truck keys in her purse.

He shrugged. "He is a smart man. If he wasn't, he wouldn't have made it as far as he did."

"And you know you guys got worked by him, right?" She gave him a sly smile.

"Oh, for sure. I think that is what bothers my brother the most." He nudged his chin in the direction of the shop. "My brother is on my ass about all this. He straight up wants me to be running down leads every second of the day. You're warned that he may bc a real ass when we get in there."

"I'm used to jackasses, in case you didn't notice."

She chuckled as they stepped out of the truck and made their way onto the sidewalk.

He went to her side, and she looked over her shoulder at the large, barred window of Lockwood Bonds. There was a big red awning over the window, which helped to keep the hot midsummer sun out of the shop, and it matched the red-and-gold stenciling on the windows. It definitely carried the German feel that had always been a cornerstone of their family's identity. The only thing missing that would have made it the perfect epitome of his family was a pint of beer and an image of broken dreams. Though maybe that was exactly what their entire shop was… broken dreams, which turned into even more broken lives, owners included.

"What's your brother's name again?" Kendra asked, stopping beside the door so he could open it for her.

"Tripp. He's a good guy, I swear, but he is just a—" He paused and gave her a guilty look.

"A ballbuster?" she said, finishing his sentence with a laugh.

He nodded.

"Then he and I should get along swimmingly."

If he agreed, he'd be an ass, but if he disagreed, he was admitting that he didn't think they'd get along. He hated these kinds of situations. "He is definitely one of those people folks either love or hate. Needless to say, he's an acquired taste, but he is one hell of a businessman. If anything, compared to him I might be the black sheep when it comes to wheeling and dealing."

"Are your parents still around?" she asked gently.

He put his hand on the brass pull as he shook his head. "They've been gone for a while now. Just he and I—but I'm the lesser brother." He laughed as he opened the door for her and followed her inside.

"You definitely are," his brother, Tripp, said, poking his head out from under the counter where he appeared to be working with something inside one of the showcases. When he spotted Kendra, he straightened up and smoothed out his shirt. "Well, hey there," he said, his voice a wicked baritone.

Trent had to withhold his desire to roll his eyes at his brother as Tripp continued to glance between him and Kendra. Tripp closed the glass showcase. Inside was a brand-new Rolex watch, no doubt an item one of their clients had used as collateral and then forfeited. "How can I help you, ma'am?"

Kendra smiled. "Well, Tripp, as your brother has graciously let me in on why he's trailing me, we need to locate Marla Thomas."

Tripp's brows rose in surprise. "Well… Ms. Spade—" Tripp said her name with a lilt of earned respect. "I find it refreshing that we don't have to dance around one another. I happen to appreciate getting life at face value for once."

Pointing at Tripp, Kendra replied, "Good. Because

you are going to be the one to flush Marla out of hiding. We need her to lead us to the senator."

"Me?" Tripp asked, rubbing his chest like her words had punched him. "How exactly do you think I could do that? I barely know her."

"Doesn't matter. But tell me something…" Kendra leaned on the case and put her fingers over the watch. "Why would Marla sign for the senator?"

Tripp dropped his hands to the edge of the glass—a little too close to Kendra's hands for Trent's liking. "She told us that it was because they worked together and she was the only friend he had left after his wife died."

"So, you knew they were having sex and you thought she was a fool in love?"

Tripp laughed as he looked at Kendra like he couldn't get enough. "Something like that."

Kendra nodded. "I'm not judging. If I was in your business, I would bet on that horse, too."

Trent suppressed a smile. He loved how Kendra was so direct and not afraid to take any situation by the balls. "What does Marla's relationship with Senator Clark have to do with flushing her out of hiding?" he asked.

Kendra sent him a sexy, bloodthirsty grin. "What would a woman who is having a relationship with a high-profile and controversial man fear the most?"

Tripp looked utterly confused. "Is this a rhetorical question or do you really want some kind of answer?

Because if you are looking for answers, I didn't pass Women 101—ask my ex-wife."

Kendra let out an audible laugh. "If any man could pass Women 101, I don't think we would be having this conversation."

Tripp snorted.

"As for what this woman fears," Kendra continued, "She doesn't want to lose the man she loves—not if she's signing a bond for a million dollars. Which means that we know what motivates her—and what we can possibly use to get her to come out of hiding."

Chapter Eight

That look, the one of shock and slight intimidation on Trent's face, was one of her favorite expressions in the world—it was exactly what she wanted her enemies to look like when she made her closing arguments in court and slammed down her fist. That being said, it wasn't an expression she wanted to see on Trent's face. Actually, she wanted to see exactly the opposite.

"My family has some connections," she said to him, "if we need to pull strings."

He didn't move; instead he looked over at his brother. "Unfortunately, Detective Baker will be dropping by here shortly to take our statements. We're supposed to be sticking around here until he does."

"Which is fine." Kendra smiled.

"Um…*what* in the hell have you two been up to?" Tripp asked, walking around so he was in complete view.

Trent began to explain the CliffsNotes version

of their eventful morning. He wasn't bad-looking, Tripp. He had the long, shaggy hair of a man who didn't have a woman in his life and probably didn't know what day of the week it was—he was likely in the shop every day anyhow, so it probably didn't matter to him unless money was due. He had the same shade of red and mahogany locks and sharp cheekbones as his brother, but he was a little longer in the face, and his nose was a touch wider. They were both handsome, but if she had to choose, there wasn't a question that she would prefer the black sheep. Yet, maybe that was her need to save a man that was once again rearing its ugly head.

The last time she had tried to save a man, it had been her ex-boyfriend. He had been a contractor for her family's company, and after an excruciating operation, one involving crimes against children, he'd lost his battle with depression and despair...a battle he'd never told her much about. She'd come to talk him down after a rambling, fast-paced series of text messages, only to have him pull a gun on her and then on himself. She had been the only one left standing, but she didn't regret trying to help him. She only wished she'd been successful.

Her fingers traced the scar.

"If I told you about our day, you wouldn't be surprised. Let's just leave it with, there was a whole hell of a lot of death and mayhem," Trent said dryly. "The senator's lawyer is dead."

"So, Clark's trial is going to be delayed? Son of a—" Tripp slammed his hand down on the wooden edge of the glass.

What? Tripp doesn't care about the lawyer? His only reaction is outrage that their man isn't going to be coming any closer to their grasp?

Kendra smirked. Yeah, they could be friends. She was an attorney, and she didn't particularly like lawyers, either—but that went mostly for defense attorneys. Then again, that was probably why she made a top-shelf prosecutor.

"Do you think Clark had a hand in the deaths?" Tripp asked.

"Presented like a murder-suicide. Looked like the attorney, Brad Bradshaw, killed his secretary, then hanged himself. But, if you ask me, it doesn't feel quite right." Trent shrugged, but she could feel his gaze work in her direction.

Trent had told the officer that she could be trusted, but from that little glance she could tell he wasn't entirely sold that she hadn't had a hand in the deaths. She felt the sudden need to affirm her truth but stopped herself from voicing it.

Yeah, she was getting entirely too *needy* about this man. She didn't have to care what he thought about her. All they needed was to get to the bottom of the deaths and get their hands on Senator Clark. Though, if he just disappeared, it would be fine by her. No lawsuit against her family. No reason to stick around. Except it would do nothing for this man she was starting to actually like.

Ugh, why do I have to feel? She nearly growled audibly at herself.

Tripp picked up his cell phone. "Let me make a few phone calls."

Kendra paused. "By chance did you guys try and get a location on Marla's phone? Find her that way?"

The men sent each other looks, like there was some kind of conversation they had already had and she'd accidentally fallen into. If there was a secret, she wasn't sure if she wanted to press the issue.

"We couldn't find a device assigned to the number she gave us, but that doesn't mean she doesn't have a phone—she probably just gave us a false number." Tripp lifted his phone as the screen was lighting up with a phone call. "I'll be right back."

Kendra nodded. There was a tall, metal stool at the far corner of the shop where it looked as though Trent had set up a little makeshift office area. A filing cabinet stood behind it, locked and inaccessible to clients, but still within view. Which made her wonder, why? Why would he want to have files out where everyone could see them? Was it his way of adding legitimacy to their trade? Some show of power, that they really did have themselves lined up? Or was it because they were so far behind that work was always right there and waiting and he needed the visual reminder?

He'd said his brother was a ballbuster about work; if they were behind or not collecting enough, it would certainly help to shed light on why this bond was critical to their survival. He'd talked a bit about the importance of it, but now she was seeing the holes in their facade of professionalism and profitability.

All their futures were on the line.

There was a *ding* as the front door opened. A tall, good-looking man with bleached tips walked in. There was a bulge under his polo shirt in the shape of a badge—it must have been Detective Baker.

"Hey," Trent said, looking at the man and giving him a friendly smile.

"How's it going in here guys?" Detective Baker glanced around the shop as he walked in. Heading to the glass showcase, he stared down at the variety of items, remnants of lives and choices that most likely led straight back to the man who was now looking at them.

For a split second, there was a knot in her stomach, as if she was nervous for the brothers. They were law-abiding men, or so she assumed, but it was always uncomfortable to fall under the scrutiny of a man who had made a life out of picking out flaws and utilizing them to his and his investigation's benefit.

Trent nodded, like he could almost read her mind, though she was certain her thoughts weren't being broadcast on her features.

"We are doing well, considering the circumstances," Trent said, motioning vaguely in the direction of the law group's office. "You here to ask us a few questions? Gotta say, I'm glad you're on the case. Nice to see a friendly face."

Baker smiled, and as he did, she noticed his canine teeth were peg-shaped. She tried not to stare at their distinctive forms. As if he had caught her looking, he closed his mouth. It made her wonder if he was insecure about them.

"My guys told me you all just happened upon the scene when you arrived for a meeting, that right?" Baker asked.

Trent moved closer to her and crossed his hands over his chest as he looked up at the detective. "Yeah, Kendra got there a few moments before I did."

"Mmm-hmm," Baker said, staring down at the case once again. He tapped on the glass like he was thinking, and the normally innocuous action made the hair on the back of her neck rise. "How long were you in there before Trent arrived, Ms. Spade?"

She sent Trent a sideways glance. "Um, I don't know. Not long, maybe a few minutes. Five or so?" Though she had done more than her fair share of taking depositions and asking suspects the tough questions, it didn't make her any more comfortable when the tough questions were being asked of her.

"We are just the ones who reported the crime," Trent said with a frown.

Baker smirked as he turned toward them. "Yeah,

you are. However, we were able to determine that the murders occurred not long before you called them in."

"Murders?" The knot returned to Kendra's stomach. "Didn't the guy hang himself?"

Baker shook his head. "Upon first inspection, one would believe so. However, it appears as if he had initially been strangled and then hung to make it look like he had taken his own life. The whole thing was, more than likely, staged." He gave them each a measured glance.

She hated the way he looked her over, peering at her, hoping to find cracks in her demeanor or any little discrepancies he could pry open like an oyster while looking for the pearl of answers. He wasn't going to be getting any answers from her, only more questions. If anything, her entire life was a series of unanswered questions smattered with the detritus of what-ifs.

"When the uniformed officers cut him loose, we found the ligature marks were inconsistent with the presentation of the body."

"And what about lividity?" Kendra asked, her mind going to the postmortem pictures she had often witnessed in her trials. How the blood pooled in a body could tell a good medical examiner or detective—even prove to a jury—the position a person had been in when they had died.

Baker sent her a wide smile, his peg teeth glinting in the late-afternoon sun. "What did you say you did for a living again?"

"I'm a prosecutor for the State of New York." She met his gaze, unafraid of detectives. She worked with them all the time, and though she understood one little misstep could land her at the top of this man's suspect list, she knew he'd see her on the same team because of her profession.

"Ah. And why were you at the law offices this morning?" Baker rubbed at the tip of his nose, a move she normally attributed to stress.

The little action made her anxiety rise, but she tried to shake the feeling by reminding herself that she was the one who held the power in this situation—she was innocent. He was the one who had to prove anything otherwise.

"I had a meeting with Brad Bradshaw about a lawsuit he and his clients had filed against my client for defamation. They were asking for a large settlement or we were to go to trial. It was my goal to find a middle ground and avoid any further legal action," she said, careful to keep her voice emotionless.

"Would you say it was to your or your client's benefit that this lawyer and his office assistant were killed today?"

She huffed and shook her head. "Absolutely not. With their unfortunate and untimely deaths, I cannot suppress the lawsuit unless I contact the lawyer's client directly. And, as luck has it, he has been working with Lockwood Bonds and recently skipped his court date and left them holding a million-dollar note, which has now been forfeited to the courts."

Baker's eyebrows rose so high that they nearly touched the edges of his blond-tipped hair. She liked his hair, if truth be told. It gave him an approachability that most detectives who she had worked with in the past lacked. "I see." He relaxed slightly, and she could feel the weight of his suspicions dissipate.

"About the murders… What was the man's cause of death?" Trent asked.

The detective stood up straight and ran his hand over his shirt, inadvertently accentuating his badge under the fabric. "Upon closer inspection, it appeared that he died from the same ligature—in this case the nylon rope—that was used to hang him from the ceiling. The initial bruising was low, here." Baker ran his finger near the base of his thick neck. "There was pooling on his back, indicating that he actually died lying down before the killer put him in the hanging position."

"Do you think the secretary could have done it?" Trent asked.

Baker shook his head. "Unfortunately, no. The gun that was likely used was found in his office and had what we believe to be her blood on the barrel. She had to have been killed first."

In most cases like these, the suspect list was generally pretty easy to put together. In her line of work, she would pull together a motive and method of the murders and what the killer had stood to gain in killing those they did—then she would hammer her points home to the judge and jury. She was proud of her ninety percent conviction rate. Yet, in this case, she found herself almost at a loss—the only ones who stood to gain anything in these deaths, at least so far as she knew, were her and her family.

One thing was certain—while she wasn't one to pull a trigger, her brothers and sister were more than happy to take down an enemy—to kill. It was their job.

Chapter Nine

After they gave the detective their statements, Trent dropped Kendra off at her ranch truck. They hadn't said more than ten words to each other since the detective left, but he didn't know exactly why— whether it was the stress of the situation or if she was just looking for the moment that she could finally get away from him and back to her life without him.

She had made it sound like they would make a great team and that they could work together to get their hands on the senator, but when he parked by her truck, she had nearly tripped over herself getting out and away from him. Kendra didn't look back at him as she got into her ranch truck, still parked in the law firm's lot.

He pulled his truck over on the side of the road and watched as she started her car and made her way out. She rolled to a stop beside him. Her eyes were tired and her jaw was set as she rolled down the window. He followed suit, expecting the permanent goodbye that was undoubtedly to come.

He steeled himself—she owed him nothing, even if he had exposed his operation to her and had come to her side when she needed someone the most in the moment. Or maybe she hadn't really needed him— maybe he just felt like he needed to be there for her.

She opened her mouth to say something, but her expression said it all—she wanted to run away to anywhere but where they found themselves. The thought made a strange sensation of refusal twist through him, its forked tongue lashing at the buried softness within him. Apparently, he wasn't as good at steeling himself against her as he wished.

Leaning in, she rested her head on the truck's steering wheel and closed her eyes.

"Are you okay?" he asked, wishing she was still just sitting next to him. It would have made it a hell of a lot easier to console her, and to ignore the fact he might never see her again.

She peeked out from under her eyelashes, and he could see the tiredness in her eyes. "I know this will sound like it comes out of nowhere, but..." She paused.

Here comes the goodbye.

He swallowed back the bitter taste of loss that crept up his throat. He had heard the adage "What is to be, shall be," but damn it if he didn't want to work to keep her in his life at least a little bit longer. Hell, he didn't even want her for his dirtiest naked fantasies—it was just nice having her around, someone smart and brave who didn't take any guff, someone he could talk to and who could confide in him.

Maybe he had just been too lonely, too long.

"Trent?" She said his name softly, like it left sweetness on her tongue that she wanted to savor.

He loved that, the sound of his name on her lips.

"Yeah, Kendra, what do you need?" He tried to say her name like she had said his, with the weightiness of want and yearning while still carrying the rasp of emotional protection he needed.

She sat up straight, and a thin smile appeared. "I know this is strange, and I don't want you to read too much into it, but I don't want to go back to the ranch. And, well… I don't really know where else to go." She sounded slightly embarrassed, like she hated exposing her underbelly to him.

He wanted to tell her it was okay to be herself with him, to show him the real her…the *soft* her that he had so far only seen in brief, sporadic glimpses.

"You can jump in with me," he offered, motioning to the passenger seat. He smiled as he realized he had been the one sitting there last. "If you want, you can even drive. I don't care."

She glanced at the parking lot and nibbled at her bottom lip. "I don't want to leave the truck here."

He wasn't sure if it was because she was afraid of the killer—who definitely wouldn't be coming for them, he hoped—or if she hated the idea of having to look upon the office of horrors, but he didn't allow himself to ask. Not every question required an answer, especially when it came to feelings. Hell, he knew only too well that he couldn't answer for what he was feeling when he looked at her; all he knew with any certainty was that he wanted more of everything she had to offer—but her time most of all.

"Why don't you drop it off at my place?" It felt strange, offering up his private dwelling to her, but at the same time, he liked the idea of her in his house... even just on his property. "You can follow me," he said, not waiting for her to shoot down the idea.

He put his truck in gear and watched to make sure she was following him before turning down the street and making his way across town. His mind wandered to his kitchen—had he left dishes in the sink? If she came inside, the last thing he wanted her to think was that he was a pig. He was pretty good about cleaning up after himself—he was the only one who was going to do it—but that didn't mean things were as picked up and put away as he would have liked in advance of a woman coming over.

There was definitely dirty laundry sitting in front of the machine. Damn, if his skivvies were sitting out, that was as good as a one-way ticket to her walking out.

He chuckled as he realized how far he had come from his days as a college student. Back then he wouldn't have thought twice about the state of his place when bringing a woman home. Then, however, he hadn't been looking for relationships. Since then, he'd learned that sex was easy. In a swipe-right culture, thanks to dating apps and instant gratification, even in a small city, there wasn't a night that had to go by when a person had to feel physically lonely...

Not that he was the kind of guy whose social calendar was filled with meaningless sex and one-night stands. In fact, he had never had a one-night stand. Lots of his friends had—even Tripp had talked about a couple—but that wasn't Trent's style.

It wasn't that he didn't like sex; he definitely did. If anything, he would say it was one of his favorite pastimes, but there was sex for sex and there was sex for love...and the latter was a whole other ballgame. There was just nothing like looking into the eyes of someone he loved and who loved him back.

It had been a long time since he had one of those moments, and with an inner wince, he remembered how he'd misinterpreted them when he was married. He'd thought his wife at the time was feeling the same things he was. He'd been wrong. She'd been silently chafing at the restrictions of marriage, and it wasn't long before she threw off what she considered its fetters. He hadn't trusted his judgment in relationships since then.

He glanced back in his mirror at Kendra, who was still following him. He doubted she was the kind of woman who liked one-night stands. And she definitely wasn't the kind of woman who opened herself up and shared herself freely. Sure, they had broken through some of the barriers of emotional vulnerability thanks to the situation in which they found themselves, but it was something else entirely to stand before another person naked both body and soul.

He still had a job to do. He needed to get his hands on the senator, or at least Marla. No matter what was or wasn't going on in his personal life, he had to make his work and his family's business as much of a priority—if not more of one. If he didn't, and they lost the business, what would he have to offer a woman?

And speaking of a woman, he thought of Kendra and how she'd let her guard down around him. He felt himself warm at the realization that she trusted him. Despite her brassy approach to life, she'd allowed him to see a softer side, a side that needed peace and normalcy.

Grabbing his phone at a red light, he did a quick search of local events. He clicked on the first one available. Apparently, there was an Iris Festival at Fort Missoula for the day, complete with food vendors, live music and dancing. He smiled at the thought of holding her in his arms and two-stepping to some good old country music. While the event could hardly make him appear to be at the top of his game, at least it was a whole heap better than showing her around his blast-from-the-past house.

Plus, Missoula was a small town, for all intents

and purposes. It was so much so that he was sure he would know at least a few of the people there. He doubted that the folks who came to him for bonds would be hanging out at a flower festival, but he could almost guarantee that their mothers and grandmothers would.

He made his way through the city, passing by mom-and-pop gas stations and roadside stands with tables filled to the edges with Russian breads and canned pickles and beets. Though he didn't have the windows open in the truck, he was sure he had caught the whiff of yeasty doughs and dill in the air as he passed by.

The park was filled with kids playing soccer in a rainbow of different colored jerseys, and there was a family reunion, marked with large signs complete with golden and white balloons, at the main pavilion. The lots were filled with cars, but toward the third row he found two spots that were next to one another and not too far a walk from the museums and garden areas.

Kendra parked and got out of her truck, but she looked confused. "What's going on? I thought we were going back to your place?"

Though he knew why he'd brought her here, he suddenly felt stupid for making the choice, and he shrugged, trying and failing to dispel some of the awkwardness he was feeling. "I thought maybe this would be better. I know you are tired and need a spot to leave your truck."

Her eyes softened, and she gave him a graceful smile. "I appreciate that, Trent."

With an acknowledging tip of the head, he wished she would reach over and touch him or take his hand and they could pretend, for at least a few moments, that they were here as a couple enjoying the summer day instead of running away from horrors and the families.

As they walked, their fingers bumped gently against one another in a way that made him wonder if she was doing it on purpose or if he was just looking for signs that weren't really there. Her fingertips brushed against his again, this time making him glance down. Her fingers were tilted slightly up; she had to be doing it on purpose—sending him a signal. And yet, why? He both feared and found himself exhilarated by the possibilities that came with this simple touch.

He smiled as he thought of what Tripp would say if his brother could see him swooning over her. Tripp had a reach-for-the-stars mentality when it came to women. He chuckled, and as he did, for a split second he forgot about his feelings of inadequacy and his fingers took hold of hers.

Realizing what he had just done, he tried to play it cool and relaxed, but his heart thrashed like a caged jackrabbit. There was no way she was going to keep her hand in his. He tried to grip just an increment tighter without her noticing. Then he relaxed his hand; he didn't need to hold her to make her stay with him. If she wanted him, she *wanted* him, and if she didn't…well, he would have to resign himself to the fate of knowing what a special woman he had lost.

What a hell that would be.

"You didn't get much of your lunch. If you want, we can get some dinner and then make our way around the gardens." He pointed at the signs, which read 89th Annual Iris Festival, and listed the hosts and sponsors below. "There's supposed to even be a band playing tonight. I think it is Stomping Ground. You like to dance?"

She gave him a look that rested halfway between *"have you lost your mind"* and *"you're crazy if you don't ask."*

"Is that look a yes or a no?" he asked, grinning at her.

"That's an *'I haven't danced to country* music' look," she said with a lightness in her voice. "I'm up for it, if you are willing to teach a girl with two left feet."

Things were looking brighter by the minute. He would dance her all the way to the moon if she would just keep touching him, but he was afraid he would sound stupid saying anything remotely close to that aloud to her.

"I'm not much of a two-stepping cowboy, but I'll

be happy to let you stomp on my toes." He gave her hand a gentle, teasing squeeze. As he did, she looked down at their entwined hands, making the happiness he was feeling teeter on the cliff of despair.

Instead of pulling away, though, she readjusted her hand so now even their palms were touching. Her hand was warm and damp with sweat, but it fit in his perfectly.

They made their way to the outlying booths of the gardening festival, complete with displays—everything from weed-mitigation strategies and companies to a stand filled with kitschy watering cans shaped like fat giraffes and squat toads.

"I miss living somewhere I could have a garden," Kendra said as they made their way past a booth filled with cut irises ranging from white to speckled purples and yellows.

Before now, he'd always thought of his grandmother when he saw the flowers. She'd had them out on the edge of the back pasture, brown and purple flowers on tall stalks and reminiscent of bygone days. Whenever he looked out at them from his kitchen window, where he'd often found his grandmother standing, he would always think of her talking about how they were the only things the *damned deer* wouldn't eat.

What she often failed to mention was the fact that she put out all her vegetable and fruit table scraps so the deer could come by and have a nibble on their nightly rounds. In fact, his grandmother had gotten so fond of the *damned deer* that one year, when a fawn had gotten caught up in their fencing around the pasture and the mother had abandoned it, his grandmother had taken to bottle-feeding it in the barn. She'd put on a heat lamp for the little spotted fawn and eventually named the baby Clem, short for clematis. Oddly enough, her deer had acquired a taste for those flowers.

"You're being quiet," Kendra said as they made their way to the next booth. "You okay? What are you thinking about?" Her mouth clamped shut as if she resented herself for asking the question. "I didn't mean to pry. I just—"

"It's okay," he said, running his thumb over the back of her hand gently to reassure her. "It's not a bad thing to be curious or to want to ask me questions. I'm one of those weird dudes who is comfortable talking about what I'm thinking…hell, even what I'm feeling on occasion."

There was that look again, like she wasn't totally buying what he was selling.

"Really, I'm comfortable not being a stereotypical dude." He hoped that being his true self wasn't going to turn her off, but he was too old to play games and pretend to be someone he wasn't in order to make the other person happy—he'd had that kind of thing in the past and it had gone out in a blaze of glory, including her slapping him so hard he was sure he'd skipped back in the week. Relationships were only truly feasible when both partners were being their authentic selves.

"I would say you have to prove that to me, but the fact that you're even willing to talk about your feelings already does that." She nudged his shoulder with hers. "You know, Trent, you are good people." There was an unexpected warmth in her voice as she looked up at him and smiled. "What happened this morning—it shook up even someone like me, who's seen and heard a lot. You knew that and have been kind to me. Kindness is rare."

"I don't know that I'm good, but I try hard to be," he said as they walked. "The thing about my line of work is that there are a lot of sleazy people who do it. I run up against that stigma all the time. I am trying to do something different, though—be in the business of helping people and not taking advantage of them when they are already at a low point."

She reached over with her other hand and held on to his arm, like suddenly she couldn't get close enough to him. "That is admirable."

His face warmed, but not just from the sun. "I still brush up against a lot of the worst kinds of people. I have to be tough enough to stand my ground and not be pushed around. Sometimes that involves more than my fair share of violence, but I try to steer clear."

She let go of his arm, and her gaze moved toward

the ground. There it was, the look of discomfort he'd been expecting when she finally really got to know him, just like with his ex. He girded himself but kept holding her hand.

Instead of letting go of him completely and moving away, she put her hand back on him. "Sometimes the only answer to violence is violence."

There was a long pause as he thought of her words and what they said about her, and her past. There was so much he still didn't know.

"I'm surprised to hear a lawyer say something like that," he said, breaking the silence. The smell of warm funnel cakes permeated the air, the sweet, warm aroma in direct opposition to their cold reality.

"Why? I can pontificate on how important a safe and just community is to American society. But at the end of the day, results are the same. Violence still occurs, people still get hurt and I find myself back in court."

He didn't disagree with how she was feeling. People, at the basic level, were animals. Many worked off impulse and survival rather than any other cognitive function. He could understand how she would get burned out on fighting what she'd made clear was a losing battle.

"At least you're making a difference. You're putting those who should be behind bars right where they need to be."

"You can't tell me you're not doing exactly the

same thing, just in a different way…a way I would never be capable of. I can land a punch and stop someone from hurting me if push comes to shove, but I'm not going to go out there and actively pursue a physical fight."

He chuckled softly, remembering her punching the man at the bar. She must have had the same thought and smiled.

"That fellow at the steakhouse was hurting me," she said in her defense, "and would have kept at it if I hadn't stopped him."

"I'm not judging. I was impressed."

"Hey," she said, letting go of him and staring ahead. "Look at that guy." She pointed into the crowd. In the distance, standing near the beer garden, was a dark-haired man with gray at his temples. He had a strong chin, and sunglasses hid his eyes. "He looks exactly like Senator Clark…" She said the name in barely more than a whisper. "You don't think he would be here, do you?"

If he'd had a warrant out for his arrest and was a recognizable and somewhat notorious public figure, the last thing Trent would have done was go to a public event. Then again, people never ceased to surprise him.

Kendra started to move in the direction of the man, just as he turned away from them and started to disappear back into the crowd of the festival. "No, don't go after him," Trent said, stopping her. "We don't want to rush headfirst into this fight."

She motioned in the direction of the senator. "If I can just talk to him, negotiate… I can put an end to the lawsuit and be on my way. We can take him to the jail, and you and your brother can get your money—plus what's owed."

There was an edge of sadness to the realization that she was right. Just like that, and their time together could be over. She could disappear back into her life in New York, and he could start hunting the next person on the list of people who had done his family wrong.

Though he knew he had a duty and he had to do the right thing, he had never wanted to do the wrong thing more… He wanted to keep Kendra by his side for at least a little bit longer.

Chapter Ten

Though Kendra had seen only a few pictures of Senator Dean Clark, she was nearly positive the man who had just disappeared into the crowd was one and the same. It was hard to mistake the plastic smile that seemed to adorn all the microdermabraded, Botoxed, filler-ridden faces of professional politicians.

At the last Met gala she had attended, she had rubbed shoulders with a former New York senator, and his personality had been more sickening and cloying than his pepper-and-sandalwood cologne. No matter how many showers she took, Kendra hadn't been able to wash the scent or the memory of the man from her mind. That night, the politician had given a small speech about the power of reform and the value of community—while later it had been rumored he had been bedding a Russian operatic soprano in one of the many utility closets.

It wasn't the first talk of his philandering ways and it wasn't the last, but his touting virtuous living and then slipping himself into every woman who would let him in their panties was a level of hypocrisy she would always find morally repugnant. From what she'd read about Clark, he was cut from the same cloth, having allegedly paid for his young daughter and wife's kidnapping, which had ultimately resulted in his wife's death. While he claimed he wasn't responsible for the crimes, a jury of his peers might decide otherwise. She believed in the principle of innocent until proven guilty, but she'd seen enough men and women like him on trial to sense where his case was headed. She assumed he was as guilty as her family proclaimed.

Trent was gripping her hand tightly as she stepped toward the senator, and there was a reticence in the way he faltered behind her, almost pulling her away from the man who could make both of their lives go back to normal. She stopped and turned to Trent.

There was a softness in his eyes, and the way the corners of his lips were raised almost gave him a pleading look. When she glanced away and then turned back, that expression had disappeared, masked by the stony front she had first noticed when she had met him. In her turning away at his beckoning softness, it was as if they had gone back to being strangers.

Instantly, she regretted her move. Just as quickly, she had to ask herself why. That kind of closeness with another person wasn't something she had ever really allowed herself to feel. When her ex had pulled the trigger, he had left her with six soul-crushing words: "You will never have true love." She would have rather felt the heat of the bullet than hear those words again.

She'd thought she'd shrugged them off at the time, the last desperate utterances of a desperate man in the throes of mental anguish.

But as time moved on, they haunted her, and it seemed he'd really murmured the phrase to the universe, not specifically to her, directing the fates to make his last wish come true. If he'd said, "You won't find anyone as good as me," she could have easily forgotten it, shaken her head over it. But the words *never* coupled with *true love* seemed to hang over her life after that incident, tainting any relationship or promise of one, making her afraid to pursue closeness.

With Trent, there was something inside her that drew her closer to him, that made her want to spend time with him, get to know him. Maybe it wasn't true love, but it was far better than any moment with her ex.

Standing there, feeling the wisp of possibility dissipate into the sky like a lonely cloud in a hot summer sky, she had to accept her ex's words for what they were—a curse.

"Trent—" She said his name with a tenderness which made the world disappear around them. "We need to go after him. If we take him down…we have the freedom to make any choices we want." She chose her words carefully, giving them just enough inflection that she hoped he understood what they really meant while being retractable if she read this moment wrong.

A smile erupted over his features, and it made a current run through her, filling her with joy. She clenched his hand tighter and almost skipped as she wove through the crowd in pursuit of the senator.

She stopped for a moment and turned, coming back to reality instead of the promises of what the future could bring. "Do you have the power to make the arrest or do we need to call in a uniformed officer?"

"I can arrest him. Besides, if we call the police, we will probably lose him before they get here." He reached down and lifted his shirt slightly so she could see the set of cuffs in a case next to his sidearm.

He walked ahead of her, letting go of her hand as he passed by. Pulling out his cuffs, he hid them in his palm so quickly and quietly that if she hadn't been watching, she wouldn't have noticed. He strode with confidence and quiet strength, a man who knew his mission. Glancing around, she looked to see if anyone in the crowd had noticed, but everyone near them was busy talking and drinking beer and wrapped up in the comings and goings of their own lives. She felt a private connection to Trent in the swirl of the crowd, a silent intimacy.

The senator's brunet head was turned from them and was moving farther away as they tried to gain ground. She was tempted to call the man's name just to slow him down and make him turn, but instead she simply followed Trent's lead. He was the point on this operation, and as such, she just needed to be there to support and call the police if things escalated.

Her throat tightened as she fell back a few steps. If this went wrong and something happened to Trent, she wasn't sure she could emotionally handle it. Not after this morning. Not after realizing how she needed to prove her ex had not cursed her.

She could put on a front like she was strong and completely unflappable regardless of what life threw at her, but she couldn't deny how shaken she was by just the thought of him getting hurt.

She stood still and watched as he reached down and rested his free hand on his sidearm, ever so inconspicuously. It was like he was dancing through the crowd, carefully moving and twisting in the way he readied himself for the battle that was likely to come.

The senator wasn't a man who would go peacefully or without a scene. The fact he had allegedly been willing to use his wife's abduction and death to help win favor with voters and appeal to their pity was only more evidence that he was total scum. Hopefully Trent realized that as well, and he was prepared for the worst.

HUNTING A PERSON was one of the strangest sensations in the world. It was thrilling and exhilarating, knowing that in just a few moments, he would be taking down his prey. Yet, this time there was a different edge to the stalk, knowing the woman he was intrigued by was only a few feet behind him.

Taking down a fugitive was one of his favorite parts of the job, but if Kendra was put in harm's way...

Trent moved faster through the crowd, hoping to create more distance between them while still not making it obvious that he was trying to leave her behind. Kendra likely wouldn't take being left in the lurch well—even if he was doing it to protect her. She'd grown up in a world of militants and violence, so she wasn't new to his world, but it was another thing entirely to see him take down a fugitive in the middle of an American park on a warm early-summer day with kids running around while chomping on shaved ice. He had to be careful.

The festival had a hometown feel, complete with the scent of hot dogs cooking on the grill mixed with the warm, yeasty odor of spilled beer. If he took down Senator Clark, he wasn't sure who would look bad—the senator or himself. He'd probably be caught on someone's camera phone doing the grab, and the senator still had fans in the public. He'd be lucky if a well-meaning passerby didn't jump into the fray and try to kick his ass in an effort to protect the pol.

He moved around the side of the man, careful to keep out of sight lines until the last moment. He wanted to take him by surprise to lower the chances of violent resistance. There didn't need to be a scene. If things went as he hoped, Senator Clark would come along willingly, without him needing to place him in cuffs or take him to the ground at all.

Approaching, he could make out the back of the man's blue polo shirt. He was talking to a woman and gesticulating with his hands to drive home whatever point he must have been making. The woman looked like she had been prisoner to the man's tirade for far too long. If nothing else, at least Trent could save this woman from further annoyance.

As he stepped within a few arm lengths of the man, he paused. As of yet, he had barely caught a glimpse of the fellow's face. Kendra had seemed to think this was definitely the senator, but now that he was closer, he could make out the man's well-kept beard. It wasn't long, but the man he and Tripp had posted for had been clean shaven and the type who went to nail salons for manicures and hadn't stepped into an ordinary barbershop in his entire life.

If we've been following the wrong man...

He nearly shook his head, but then a part of him secretly hoped that they had made a mistake and were going after the wrong person. It would be easier when it came to this *thing* that was happening between Kendra and him. If they were barking up the wrong tree, they would have to keep looking. Which meant they could have more time together—time when she could come to her senses and realize that she was a million times too good for him. Until she did, he was going to soak up every second.

The man he had been tailing started to move toward the stage where a country band was playing a ballad perfect for dancing. The man took the annoyed woman's hand and she resisted for a moment, but he refused to let go. The woman jerked her arm back, trying to break the grip, but the action only made the man's hand tighten, and her skin around his fingers turned white from the pressure.

This was Trent's moment. He moved quickly, cutting off the man's path to the patch of grass that was acting as the dance floor. There were a few dozen couples out there; one of the men was whispering something into his partner's ear, and his date had a nearly blinding smile.

It was a sharp contrast to the imprisoned expression on the face of the blonde who was accompanying their target. He stared at the man's features. His face was obscured by sunglasses and the beard, but he was almost certain the man was Dean Clark. Trent chastised himself for thinking he could have been anyone else. He had apparently come here in this pitiful attempt at a disguise to meet Marla.

Did she know the kind of man who she had laid down her financial future for, the same man who had strapped her with a million-dollar debt because he couldn't face the judge and answer for his alleged crimes?

"Mr. Clark?" he said, stepping directly in front of the bearded man.

As Dean heard his name, he jerked and glared at Trent, like he was trying to place his features.

Dean let go of the woman's arm and her hand moved to where he had been holding her, but not before Trent caught sight of the dark pink lines Dean's fingers had left on her skin.

He would have hated this man even if he didn't owe Trent money. No woman should be treated the way he had been treating her.

"Who the hell are you?" Dean growled, moving behind his date.

The blonde's face relaxed and she moved to step away from Dean, but he put his hands on her shoulders and forced her to stay put.

What kind of lies had Dean told this woman to get her to go out with him?

"Ma'am, do you feel safe?" Trent asked, and he looked over the senator's shoulder to Kendra, who had finally pushed her way through the crowd.

She looked slightly annoyed that he had left her behind, but as she spotted him, the annoyance slipped from her face and was replaced with a quizzical expression of concern.

The blonde with the senator reached up and removed his left hand and then his right from her shoulders. "Actually, I could use a ride so I can get out of here."

Trent nodded and motioned for Kendra to come closer. "My friend Kendra here will be happy to take you anywhere you need to go." He was happy to do anything that could save this seemingly innocent woman from the grips of an accused murderer who lacked any sort of conscience.

Kendra gently put her hand on the woman's back and waved her hand away from the stage and the throngs of people, several of whom had suddenly appeared to have taken notice of what was threatening to take place.

"Tracy, you stay right there. Damn it," Dean ordered, reaching to take hold of the woman again.

So, this wasn't Marla with him. Of course not. The man was a philanderer and this must have been just another of his many women, but this one was just at the wrong place at the wrong time.

The woman lurched away from Dean's grasp.

"Kendra, get her out of here," Trent said, trying to keep his voice even but firm. He needed both women to get out of here before something really bad happened. He couldn't risk them getting hurt—even if he was more than aware Kendra was strong enough to kick some ass.

"I don't know who in the hell you think you are,

but you and that little snatch you're with need to mind your own goddamned business," Dean said.

Trent let out a dark laugh. The man had found it— he had found his crazy switch, the one that flipped him from a person who could open up and talk about his feelings into someone not afraid to kick ass and take names. No one would talk about Kendra that way.

No effing way.

As if Kendra could see the steam that was roiling out of his ears, she grabbed the blonde and began leading her back toward the truck.

"You stop right there," Dean yelled. As he did, the song came to an end and his voice broke the lull between the tunes.

Every face in the area turned toward them and the scene that the senator was creating.

Kendra didn't even look back, but the blonde paused. Kendra shook her head and said something. Trent couldn't quite make out all the words, but they sounded like, "Don't go back to him." Trent hoped they worked. There was nothing worse than watching a person whose spirit had been broken down by a toxic and abusive partner.

"I don't know if you recall, but recently you were ordered to appear in court and failed to, leaving Lockwood Bonds holding the bag for more than a million dollars, plus interest," he said to the senator.

Dean pulled up his sunglasses, putting them on

his head as he looked around at the crowd of people that had formed around them. "I have no idea what you are talking about."

"Senator Clark, while I'm sure it was merely an oversight on your part, missing your court date…" He spoke slowly, measuring his words and their effects on the crowd like they were drops of a poisonous elixir. "You know, the felony criminal proceedings for your role in your daughter's kidnapping—a daughter you no longer have custody of—and your wife's kidnapping and murder."

The man's face blanched, and a bead of sweat worked its way down from his hairline and onto his temple; even from where he stood Trent could see the vein protruding beneath it. "I had nothing to do with any of that. And I don't know what court date you are talking about."

"See, I'm sure it is all a misunderstanding, Senator. You just need to come with me and we will sort it all out."

The man's eyes widened—*rabbit eyes* were what he and his brother called them. Dean reached down and touched his shorts like he was going to tighten them, and then he looked the way Kendra and the blonde had gone and around to where there was a small opening in the crowd of people. He was going to run. Trent could sense it.

Trent leaned toward the man, saying lowly in an effort not to cause a scene, "Don't do it. I'll catch you, and when I do, there will be an ass whooping at the end of it."

The man looked him over, like he was considering how bad the beating would be. "Look, I don't know who you think you are, but I can assure you that as a senator I'm an upstanding citizen in this community."

Trent raised his hand, stopping the man's canned garbage speech. "We can stand here and hash this out here in front of all these witnesses, or you can come with me and we can discuss this in private."

The man flexed his hands and balled them into fists, giving him the look of a petulant child.

Trent opened his hand and exposed the cuffs resting in his palm in hopes of avoiding violence. "If you come with me nicely, I won't put these on you…"

He took a step closer, but as he did the man's fist came out of nowhere, and Trent cursed himself for being too trusting as he'd tried to avoid a scene. Before he could react, he felt the crush of bone on bone as the senator's fist connected with his temple. His ears buzzed and a strange floating sensation moved through him. Trent tried to move, to swing in retaliation, but his movements felt like they were being repressed by the tides.

The second hit, a roundhouse, he saw coming. There was nothing his dazed body could do except try to block, but he moved too slowly, and as the hit struck, he knew…he was going down.

Chapter Eleven

From the living room of her hotel suite, Kendra could make out the sounds of sheets rustling on the couch—Trent must have been waking up. Last night, after she had picked Trent up at the hospital, she hadn't wanted to take him back to her family's ranch, and he hadn't wanted to go home.

After the attack yesterday, she'd wanted to be alone, away from his brother and her family, the people who had set them on this course. They needed room to sort out what was going on, how the pieces of their separate cases fit together.

She had lived in many hotels over the years, and the DoubleTree was pretty typical of the nicer ones in which she had resided. She always went for the upgrade at hotels, slipping the front desk staff twenty bucks when she handed them her ID just so she could get a better room. This time it had definitely worked—they had given her the presidential suite. It probably hadn't hurt that she'd had Trent on her arm, black eye and all.

He had definitely taken one hell of a hit. As much as she had known that the senator could cause a scene, she hadn't expected the politician to actually resort to blows. She was as surprised as Trent had been. He'd obviously been working hard to keep the situation under control so that no one would get hurt. He was a good man, so he'd ended up getting hurt himself.

The senator's move seemed out of character. However, this morning social media had blown up and the video of Trent getting the beatdown had gone viral—so far, it had more than three million views. Hopefully one of them was Marla. If the senator was going to keep slipping out of their grip, then they were definitely going to have to focus more on the woman who had cosigned for him. At least, she could act as an insurance policy.

The good news was that, thanks to the video, she could very likely use it against the senator in the event that the lawsuit continued. As it was, she could definitely use it to her family's benefit. The senator was a loose cannon—a man who cared nothing about the safety and welfare of others but was solely focused on himself.

If nothing else, she could thank Trent for taking one for her family's team. The video and propaganda rolled in her favor, and it was always a welcome gift. It wouldn't guarantee a win, but it would make getting one significantly easier. That was, if they even ended up making it to court—as things were going, if the senator didn't make it to the criminal proceedings with a new legal team, well…he definitely wouldn't be following through with his civil action against her family. It had been a ballsy move for him to even file the civil claim before the criminal trial. Usually defamation cases came after not-guilty verdicts, aimed at those who'd painted the defendant as guilty as sin from the get-go.

This case was more complicated than she'd first imagined.

Which once again led her to wonder how and why someone had gone after his lawyer. Now that they knew the senator had likely been in town when the murders had taken place, it put him higher up on the suspect list. Maybe the man was more than just ballsy. Maybe he was relentless in taking down people in his way.

By now Detective Baker had to be aware of the video floating around on social media, and she was surprised they hadn't gotten a phone call or a visit from him. Heck, it was a small enough town that if he wanted to track them down at this hotel, he certainly could have by now.

Perhaps that meant the detective was thinking the same thing she was and was currently on the lookout for the senator in hopes that he could bring him in for questioning about his attorney's demise.

The television in the other room clicked on, and

Kendra pulled her hair back and slipped on the white robe that came with the room. Making her way out, she was taken aback when she spotted Trent. He was shirtless, leaning back into the corner of the L-shaped couch, a sheet covering his lower body. He had his arm up, his hand behind his head, and the other hand was lying just under the edge of the sheet on his abs. His biceps were enormous, and a cobra tattooed in black ink wrapped around one of them.

Just when she thought he couldn't get any hotter and she was in fear for her virtue, he looked over at her and sent her a sleepy smile. "I hope I didn't wake you." His eye had taken on a red ring around the iris, and his cheek was still swollen and covered in a black-purple bruise.

She wanted to go to him and run her finger over the bruise and kiss it until it was better, but she resisted the urge. It was already embarrassing to be standing here in front of him in a bathrobe and staring like a lust-filled teenager who was just experiencing her first real crush.

"No," she said, her voice raspy from the morning. She cleared her throat. "I need some coffee, though. You?"

"I'm not a coffee drinker, but if you want, I can get up and make you a cup or go for a coffee run or something." He really looked at her now, and she could feel his gaze move down her like it was his hands skimming over her body.

Yep, he was getting hotter by the passing second. Any man who made coffee for his woman deserved a special place in the bedroom—and any position he wanted.

She smiled at the thought of opening up her robe and letting it fall to the floor in front of him. What would he do?

All of a sudden, needing coffee was drifting from her mind.

He smirked. "You look beautiful this morning. Do you know that?"

She put her hand up to her hair, fussing with a strand that she had forgotten to secure in her bun. "Thank you for the compliment." She paused. Did she throw the bait or did she just take the compliment and retreat? "Though I can't say I probably look half as sexy as you."

She was met with only the sounds of ESPN for a long moment—some team somewhere had won something—but all the words were melting together in a jumble as she thought about the mistake she had just made. It was never a good idea to make the first real move with a man. She had made the first move with her ex, demonstrating that if left to her own devices she always picked the wrong men.

Reaching down, she pulled the edge of the robe tighter, wishing she could disappear into it and end up as just a heap of puffy white cotton on the floor.

"Why are you doing that?" he asked, voicing the

question going through her own mind. "If anything, you should come over here, closer to me." He patted the couch next to him. There was a yearning in his eyes, a look of wanting she hadn't seen in him before.

She started to move toward the couch, her walk slow and deliberate.

As she got close to him, he reached out for her hand, motioning to her as if it was an invitation. Yet she had been the one to invite. She slipped her fingers in his, and he pulled her to him in one smooth action.

"When I'm around you, I'm never quite sure why I'm doing anything," she said with a whisper of a smile. "And I'm usually pretty decisive."

"What are you deciding now?" he asked, so softly she barely heard him.

"That I want you, and I suspect you want me." There was something about Trent that called for complete honesty, and she liked the feeling of being able to say what was in her heart and mind.

"How long have you known that I wanted you?" He lifted her hand to his mouth and kissed her open palm, making her knees weaken.

"It doesn't matter to me who wanted who first. I'm just glad to be here with you now." She sucked in a breath as he moved her palm to his cheek and reached around her, wrapping her in his arm.

"You're one of the smartest people I've ever met, do you know that?"

Though she enjoyed being called beautiful, being called intelligent turned her on far more. Being beautiful was nothing more than getting lucky in the genetic draw—that or entirely too much makeup. Intelligence took years of hard work and diligence to acquire, and even then it wasn't a guarantee. She had known many people who graduated from college but couldn't find their way out of a hotel bathroom.

"If you're trying to butter me up, it's working." She smiled at him as she reached up and ran her fingers through his soft reddish-brown hair.

"Are you sure?" Trent asked.

She twisted a lock of his hair between her fingers as she looked at him, confused by his question. "Of course I am. Why do you ask?"

He gave her a devious grin, his eyes sparkling. He reached up with his other arm and pulled her into his lap, exposing her legs almost to her panty line.

"I ask, because if I was doing this right, you would already be kissing me."

Her fingers slipped from his hair down to his sharp jawline, and she slowly moved toward his lips, staring at the sweet pinkness and the lines that adorned them.

The first kiss was dangerous. There were so few of them in life, ones that mattered. As wonderful as a first kiss could be, for her it always carried an air of sadness. No first kiss had ever lasted long enough. Nor had any of them led to promises of forever. In essence the first kiss was acknowledging temporary bliss and future heartbreak. Even acknowledging that this would almost inevitably lead to nothing, she still couldn't resist Trent. They'd met during a moment of heightened awareness, at the scene of a murder, and ended the day in a moment of heightened tenderness as she'd cared for his bruises. She would have to have a heart of steel enclosed in ice to resist their pull toward each other.

To make this step, and take things between them further, was an enormous gamble. She stopped moving long enough to look him in the eyes. There was no deceit, no hints of broken promises or inconsistency. As he looked at her, she only saw wanting and whispers of what *could be*.

He leaned in, taking her lips and not allowing her to overthink anymore. She wrapped her arms around his neck, holding him close as she savored the flavor of his kiss. Though he'd just woken up, he tasted of toothpaste and promises.

His kiss was luxurious and unhurried, his tongue flipping over her lip gently and reminding her of the sensation of butterfly wings. She could remember no more sensual sensation than when he moved against her. She didn't know how his hand had found her face, but he pushed a wayward hair from the corner of her mouth and let his thumb linger on her cheek.

She was tempted to open her eyes to see the man who was sweeping her away and making her forget about everything and every responsibility. All she could think about was how it felt so good to be kissed by him. To be kissed like he meant it. Like she was his. She kissed him back with the same gentle seriousness. She wanted him to be hers.

This kiss…could it mean forever? She pushed that thought away and lost herself in him.

His breath was warm against her skin, and it reminded her of how the sun felt after a long, harsh winter. She couldn't deny that that was what her life had been right up to this moment—a cold season filled with struggle. In this second, she didn't have to be the strong one.

It was refreshing and freeing to let go of all the pressure and requirements that her life entailed.

Too quickly, he broke away from their kiss. His hands lingered on her face, as did his gaze. His eyes were wide and round, soft, as he looked upon her. She could have melted. Though he didn't say the words, she could feel there was something more to the look than simply lust. In him, she could see a future of languid bliss and relaxed and passionate adventures. If she was right, he was everything she'd ever looked for in a partner.

As much as she wanted him to tell her that he cared for her, to hear endearments that indicated this was more than just quick passion soothing two troubled hearts, she hesitated. There was no need to rush—there was a certain beauty in being patient and enjoying each moment together in this room. As soon as they stepped outside, life would come rushing at them from every direction.

"You are *so* unexpected. You are so different than the man I first thought you were. You are so smart and…so incredibly kind." She didn't dare say what she was thinking—that she would love to dream of a forever with him. A statement like that, in a moment like this, would have exactly the opposite effect than what she wanted. If someone said something like that to her, it would be a giant red flag.

Given how she was feeling, though, she had to question her assumptions and judgments about falling into anything resembling love at first sight. Technically, this wasn't at first sight, but it was close enough. Everything in her life she had made intentionally slow; it saved a person from making impulsive decisions that would inevitably come back to haunt them.

With Trent, however, it felt different. The idea that she could fall in with loving didn't feel impulsive. If anything, it felt complementary. He evened her out and balanced her in ways that she had never experienced with a partner before. He seemed to allow her to work through her feelings without feeling rushed, but at the same time, there was hunger and an unspoken invitation.

Taking his hand in hers and saying nothing, she moved the top of her robe aside and put their entwined hands over her heart. She wanted to tell him that in this moment, her heart beat for him and she would carry him there forever, regardless of what happened in their relationship.

This kind of moment, one in which she was giving herself freely to him, it wasn't something she ever did. Before now, whenever she had been with a man, she had been able to give her body but not her soul. None of the men she'd ever been with deserved to see the real her. She'd feared giving them access to who she really was, because in doing so she also handed them the golden ticket to destroying her.

Hopefully she wasn't making a mistake.

More, she hoped he understood in her simple touch, what she was leaving unspoken—that she trusted him and so much more.

He ran his fingertips over the scar just below her collarbone. "What happened here?" He moved closer, kissing the dimpled skin that carried so much of the past in its ridges and valleys.

She touched his face gently, looking into his big eyes. "I was shot…but it wasn't anything as exciting as what you think," she added quickly as he pulled back.

"What? When? How?" He looked angry and at war with himself as he stared at the scar.

"An ex thought if he didn't have me, no one else should, either… It's why I left him and my family business. I had to run. This life—the people in it, the world around it—wasn't for me. The only way I was going to stay alive and make a difference was by fighting for what was right in the courtroom."

"I am so sorry." He paused. "I know that's not what you want—pity—but I'm sorry that you ever had to go through that. I wish I had found you sooner, stopped that from ever happening."

Her eyes welled with tears as she looked at him. She loved this man's soul. He was so beautiful inside and out.

"Do you know what you do to me, when you look at me like that?" Trent traced the shape of a heart on her delicate skin.

She opened her legs slightly, exposing her lacy black panties.

Trent sucked in a breath, and his fingertips slipped on her skin and moved to the intersection of her thighs. He gently stroked the tender nub at her center. She moaned, closing her eyes as she tilted her head back and enjoyed the sensation of him pleasuring her.

His fingers moved faster, spinning circles on her in all the right ways. It was like he knew exactly what she needed, and there was a comfort with him, as if they had spent many a night together in bed. She wasn't sure why she felt as she did with him; it normally took months of getting to know a man before she could be this comfortable.

He gave her hope that he could bring her to completion. When it came to sexual satisfaction, she wasn't an easy lock to pick. Maybe she was too much in her own head, or maybe it was the controlling aspect of her personality, but releasing for a man was always a challenge.

"Kendra." He spoke her name gently, as gentle as his fingertips felt below.

"Yes?" she whispered between breaths.

"Relax for me." He moved closer to her neck as he spoke, and the words caressed her skin as seductively as his tongue had moved against her bottom lip.

The words in combination with his touch made her grow impossibly wetter. She wanted him. She wanted more than simply his fingers moving over her panties. "Please," she begged.

He shook his head and brushed her hair from her neck as he swirled his fingers faster. He gently kissed the soft spot right below her earlobe, slow and in direct contrast to the speed of his fingers.

He told her to relax, but something inside her was building. There was an ache for him and an ache for something else… Something deeper.

She wanted everything.

His lips trailed down her neck over the top of her shoulder as he pulled back her bathrobe, and it slipped down her arm, exposing her hardened nipples. He kissed along the top of her shoulder as his free hand stroked her breast. She gasped at the intensity of everything he was making her feel—hot and cool, hard and soft, rough and tender.

He moved to the other side, exposing her completely. The only thing keeping the robe on her was the thin tie around her midsection.

As the pressure to release mounted, there was a knock at the door.

She jumped up, closing her robe tightly around her.

"I'll get it," he said, nodding for her to head to the bedroom. She rushed there, slamming the door behind her. It was a slight overreaction to a silly knock at the door, but she felt like a teenager who just been caught making out by her parents.

Everything…it had all happened so fast. This wasn't her style, and it left her feeling completely off kilter.

From the living room, she heard Trent get up from the couch. There was the click of the peephole opening and closing and then the slide of the latch.

"Is my sister here?" AJ asked.

She had no idea how he had found her, but his being here made her feel like a child who'd stayed out after curfew. Checking that her robe was completely closed, she tried to collect herself as she headed back out into the living room. AJ was standing there with his arms over his chest, looking every bit like their father.

Heat rose in her cheeks, even though she tried to keep it at bay. She was an adult woman with a career and a mind of her own. She didn't need to feel like a kid under her brother's scowl. "Why are you here, AJ?"

He looked her up and down, assessing her lack of clothing. "If you think I want to be here, seeing you in that, you couldn't be more dead-ass wrong." He waved at her with all the condemnation of an angry judge. "I'm here because you need to learn to answer your goddamned phone."

The only thing she needed to learn was how to keep from being found.

Chapter Twelve

There was embarrassed, and then there was being-called-out-by-a-brother embarrassed. Trent was used to neither. He couldn't remember a time when he had been more self-conscious than he was right then, being stripped down verbally by AJ Spade—a man he had never met.

"What do you want, AJ?" Kendra asked.

Though Kendra looked put together and willing to stand up to her brother, Trent was having one hell of a time trying to cover up his discomfort. Both physical and mental.

"I just heard about your run-in with the senator," AJ said, finally looking at Trent's face and seeing him for something more than the man who was trying to bed his sister. "You got your ass kicked."

Trent nodded. "Yeah, but your sister got the senator's date to safety." What he didn't mention was that it had also led to them being in the room where they currently were standing. If getting his ass beat meant that he got to spend one more night alone in proximity to Kendra Spade, he'd gladly take another hit.

"Did you see what was happening on social media?" AJ asked.

Kendra shook her head. "Before we get any more into this, I'm going to go get dressed."

AJ nodded. "Please do." Venom dripped from his words.

Crap. He didn't regret the direction he and Kendra had been taking things, but he didn't want to be in this room alone with AJ. Nothing good would come of that. Before he tried to come up with some excuse to get away from the man, Kendra took him by the arm. "And he'll be coming with me."

He wasn't one to be shuffled around, but for once he was glad just to follow directions. "Be right back," he said with the tilt of the head.

AJ's scowl deepened. "I'm not going to stand here and wait for you guys to do whatever it is you're gonna do. I'll meet you in the hotel lobby. You better not be more than five minutes." He turned to the door and stormed out, letting it bang shut behind him.

Kendra sighed. "Well, that was my brother AJ. And now you know why I wasn't in a hurry to go back to my family ranch."

"He is never going to like me."

Kendra shrugged. "If I was concerned about my brother and his opinion on my life, and the people I choose to bring into it, that would've given me a nonrefundable ticket to the psychiatric ward." She laughed. "You know…most people fear their fathers and the judgment of their parents, but growing up I was always most concerned with what AJ thought of me. Thankfully, I've outgrown it. Not to mention the fact that I intentionally isolated myself from this family years ago."

"I'm sure your brother loves you and only wants the best for you, and undoubtedly that includes the men you date. I just wish he and I could've gotten off to a better start." As he spoke, he realized he was referring to the future—one that he and Kendra had never even talked about.

He walked back to the chair in the corner, picking up his shirt and carefully hiding his face. Apparently, today was going to be full of embarrassments. He could hardly wait to see what the rest of it would bring. All he wanted, if he had his way, was to pull her back onto his lap to continue what they'd started. Unfortunately, that moment was gone. Knowing his luck, it was gone forever, and Kendra would soon come to her senses and leave him.

"Regardless of what you and I choose to do," she started, sounding uncomfortable in addressing what might or might not have been the start of a relationship between them, "AJ's opinion is not any of my concern. I'm going to do what makes me happy."

He liked that sentiment and the thought that he made her happy. He hoped he would get the chance to make sure the way he made her feel never changed, but the dark cloud of reality and logic loomed overhead. "You know, I think there are several things that can act as indicators of a worthwhile relationship."

Though it might not have been in his best interest to bring the subject up, he also wasn't going to censor himself. He was too old to play the games he had played when he was in college, pretending to be interested in what the woman liked and to hate whatever it was she hated. He had once gone without potato chips for almost six months to please his ex-wife—never again.

She stepped beside him. There was a frown on her face. "I'm not sure, with that look, that I want to know." She sounded like she was teasing, but he wasn't quite sure. "Tell me, though. I'm curious to know how your mind works."

He laughed. "Trust me, you probably don't."

She put her hand on his back, and there was a comfort that came with her touch; it was unexpected, but he reveled in it for a second too long and was only brought back to reality when she rubbed her finger over his shoulder blade. "I want to know everything there is to know about you." She gave a nervous laugh. "You know, so I can get a full picture of the man I'm working with."

"Working with?" he asked with the raise of a brow, thinking about how she had opened up and even revealed some of her scars.

"Just tell me what you need in a relationship."

He hadn't said he *needed* anything, merely what he believed was an indicator of something worth pursuing, but he didn't correct her. He needed to trust her, just as she had trusted him. "I think if you are dating the right person, they will help you be the best version of yourself. They will push you to your next level. Together, you should feel like you can take on the world. If they are holding you back or hurting you, in any way—" as he spoke those words, he felt a tug at his heart that told him this was probably him when it came to her "—then you should find someone better."

There was a look of pain in her expression, and her hand moved from his shoulder. "Well, I'm glad we don't have to worry about anything like that," she said, turning away and going toward her room. "I'll be right out. I'm going to finish getting myself together."

She had looked perfect to him, but then she always did, so he wasn't sure why she needed to excuse herself other than he had once again said the wrong thing. If he had made her think he was pushing her away, that hadn't been his intention at all. However, she did need to really and truly consider all that he was before she made the decision to continue down this path. He didn't want to be hurt if he gave her his all and then she came to realize he wasn't what she wanted.

Or perhaps she already knew she wasn't at her best with him, and that was why she needed a moment on her own? He took in a deep breath, trying to center himself.

He slipped into his clothes and readied himself for the day with a quick shave. Coming out of the bathroom, he took one more look at the sheet that he had left thrown on the corner of the couch. Damn AJ and damn his interruptions.

Kendra appeared, wearing a different outfit from the ranch supply store, a black Orvis skirt with a button-down white shirt. He stared at the label on the skirt, impressed that she would wear a fly-fishing brand.

"Did you grab all your stuff?" she asked, and though the question was neutral, there was the underlying implication that she wasn't planning on having him stay with her again.

He tried not to cringe. "Yep, running pretty light these days." He walked over to the side of the couch and picked up his go-bag, which always lived in the back of his truck.

"Something tells me it's not just lately. With your job, and how much you travel, you probably can pack up your whole life into a bag like that," she said, motioning toward his tactical backpack.

Without speaking, he walked to the door and held it open for her, careful to keep his bag out of the way. They strode quietly down the hall, passing door after door. From behind some, he could make out the sounds of television, children talking, and one conspicuous moan, which made him think of Kendra's hotel robe falling open. At the noise, they grinned knowingly at one another, and for a moment, her look made his heart skip a beat. Perhaps she had been brought back to the thoughts of his fingers between her legs.

Before he could decide, she was moving ahead of him down the long hallway.

The hotel lobby was quiet, a few people standing at the concierge's desk, talking with the woman there about restaurants in the area. He grimaced when he spotted AJ behind the bay window that looked out onto the Clark Fork River, which ran through the center of town. He looked just as perturbed as he had in their hotel room—so much so that Trent couldn't help but wonder if that was just AJ's normal expression.

"AJ, thank you for your patience." Kendra's voice had the sharpness of the knife Trent always carried in his pocket.

"Don't give me any of your nonsense. Everyone has been trying to call you. You should have seen Zoey. She was about to load up the baby and come here and get you herself." AJ's scowl deepened as he looked over at him. "And you must be the man of the hour. Because of you and your affiliation with my sister—thanks to the videos on the internet—

our family is being dragged through the mud. I'm not sure if you are aware of this or not, but my family isn't one that appreciates a whole lot of media attention."

"You need to stop right there, AJ," Kendra said, stepping between them. "I don't know what happened in the last twelve hours that makes you think you can barge into my hotel room and into my life and start acting like a jerk, but you need to stop. You have no right to treat me or my guest this way."

"Your *guest*?" AJ laughed. "That's one way to put it."

Kendra's dark laugh reverberated through the lobby, and the concierge and the hapless tourists stopped talking.

AJ didn't move.

"Is everything all right?" the concierge asked as she reached for the phone.

"Fine," AJ grunted, and she put down the receiver.

Trent stepped to Kendra's side in a show of support. "Why don't we talk about this outside?" he said, motioning toward the doors that led to the patio overlooking the river.

AJ shot him a look that told him he didn't appreciate being spoken to by him in the slightest, but Trent didn't care. From everything he'd seen, and what Kendra had told him, AJ could kiss his ass if he thought he could get away with treating his sister the way he had been. He had wanted to assume

AJ had her best interests at heart and wanted to do nothing more than protect her, but it appeared that perhaps the only thing AJ really cared about was making his sister come to heel.

AJ was clearly an idiot if he thought Kendra would let him get away with that kind of behavior. She was a woman with standards and boundaries that weren't drawn in sand but, rather, in concrete.

The patio was empty, thankfully. They didn't need to make any more of a spectacle of themselves. Ever since they had started working together, he and Kendra had left a wake of bloodied lips and bodies behind them—now AJ was included. Yet he would like to keep things from moving farther downhill.

"So, you were saying that there has been fallout on social media? What has been going on since last night?" Trent asked, trying to dispel some of the tension that was swarming between the siblings like wasps.

AJ cleared his throat, tore his glare away from his sister and exhaled. "First, Kendra, you are right. I do owe you an apology."

She frowned. "If you don't mean it, I wish you wouldn't even fake it. There's nothing worse than being disingenuous."

AJ smiled, apologetically. "No, really, I meant it. And if I weren't already in the doghouse, I would argue that there are several things worse than being disingenuous." He lifted his left hand, which was missing the middle finger. "For example, it's a pain in the ass not being able to flip a-holes off in traffic."

Kendra chuckled and in the sound was the balm of forgiveness. "Oranges and fingertips, hardly comparable, but I'll allow it."

"As I knew you would." AJ sent her a cheeky smile. "As for you—" AJ turned to him as he spoke, his voice taking on a dry tone "—I'm still pissed. However, I do appreciate you looking out for my sister. I know she isn't one to take directions—or criticism—well. The fact you can work with her at all says something about you."

He wasn't sure if that was a ringing endorsement of either himself or Kendra, but at least no one was slapping anyone.

"Don't ruin a good apology by being an ass, AJ," Kendra said. "Now, what is going on?"

AJ sent him one more wary glance before resigning himself to his sister's admonishment. "My apologies, Trent."

He didn't dare to ask how the man knew his name, considering Kendra had yet to actually introduce them. "No harm, no foul, man." He would take the olive branch where he could get it.

AJ dipped his head in acknowledgment. "So, Zoey might have left you several messages, but there has been a viral explosion on all the social media sites. According to the senator, your boy here—" he motioned toward him "—is being portrayed as some wacked-out religious zealot who had a vendetta against the senator."

"Are you kidding me?" Kendra growled. "Who was behind that stroke of political genius?"

"The senator and his public relations team. They know what they are doing and how to turn what could potentially have been political suicide into a boon." AJ shook his head. "If you had been more transparent with us, we could have gotten ahead of this. Now we are playing cleanup. Zoey, our boss at STEALTH—" he glanced at Trent, filling him in "—isn't pleased."

"Is there a time when Zoey is pleased?" Kendra asked.

AJ smirked, as if that was answer enough.

Trent had to bet all Kendra's siblings were like AJ. He held no doubts that they were a tough lot; given the fact that they were a group of private military contractors, they weren't going to be the kind who walked around patting each other on the backs. Yet, seeing how hard her world could be—and how it paralleled his own, but on a larger-number-of-siblings scale—he could understand her leaving them.

"How can we get on top of this?" Trent asked. He was good on tech, but he wasn't a social media hound, at least not when it came to content creation.

"How can we get the senator pinned down? Or Marla?" Kendra added. "I thought Zoey was on top of this."

AJ shrugged. "She's working on it, but there is no fixing the public perception now. That ship has sailed. Your boy is a bad guy as far as the world is concerned." He shot him a look. "Despite the criminal accusations against the senator, he still has supporters who are willing to use social media to spread his lies."

Trent was used to not being the most liked man in town, because of his job, but being hated around the world due to social media was new to him. He hoped like hell that Tripp wouldn't have to start fielding any nasty phone calls or death threats.

"Was there any mention of me being a bounty hunter?" Trent asked.

AJ shook his head. "No, like I said, they are just calling you a man who had a vendetta against the senator. He's done pretty well suppressing any details about his role in the altercation."

"Of course he has," Trent grumbled.

"Zoey is posting versions of the video with our audio. We may have made a few key adjustments and added closed captions, but it's all true, and the tide is turned away from us." AJ ran his hands over his face. "Now we just have to hope for the best and keep our name from getting out into the public too much more." AJ started to make his way toward the doors to leave.

"Wait," Kendra called after him and he turned back. "Who is Dean's criminal defense attorney, the one he is using to defend himself against the charges in his wife's death? I've only been dealing with our defamation suit."

"It's a woman named Kate Thomas. Why?"

Kendra frowned. "With Bradshaw Law Group or another firm?"

AJ paused and tapped on his phone. "Looks like she is with the Bradshaw Group."

Kendra shook her head. "I should have guessed. Where is this Kate Thomas, and why wasn't she in the office on the day of the murders?"

Chapter Thirteen

It felt ridiculously good to get back to work. Being with Trent had been more than nice, but with everything going on, it had been foolish to take things where they had. Besides, she prided herself on her ability to look toward the future; she was a planner, and being with a man who had no likelihood of moving across the country to be with her would spell nothing but disaster.

She wasn't one to believe in true love or soul mates—those kinds of romantic notions were for those who had the freedom to make mistakes. Love wasn't something she could ever really dream of having; she didn't have room in her life for a mistake as momentous as falling for the wrong person.

"Are you okay?" Trent asked, but he was looking in the direction of her hands on the steering wheel.

"I'm fine." She nodded. "I'm just thinking about the attorney Kate Thomas. I looked into her law practice, and her office is officially closed for the time being…though there was no mention of the murders."

"No surprise there. Death is bad for business." Trent's expression of concern didn't falter. "What were you thinking about Kate?"

She was relieved to be focusing back on their work instead of their burgeoning feelings, or whatever it was between them. "I am just thankful we have another way to get to the senator. Marla…she's damned near a ghost."

Trent chuffed. "No kidding. And with your brother breathing down our necks…" He shook his head. "AJ, and, well, your whole damned Spade family…you guys are *intense*."

A thought struck her as she stared out at the Western-style brick building that made up most of downtown and he spoke their last name. They came to a stop at the light. "Did it occur to you Marla's last name is also Thomas?"

He scratched at the back of his neck. "Well, now that you mention it. It's a fairly common name, though. You think they're related or something?"

She put her hands up, shrugging. "It's something worth looking into. A defense attorney's unlikely to share much information with us, but we should try."

"Yeah," he said with a resigned sigh, like he could feel how desperate she was to grasp at straws. "Ever since…well, *you know*…back at the hotel…things have been off. Is there anything I can do make things right with us, or at least make it easier between you and your brother?"

The red light lasted forever.

She had a number of options as to how she could tell him there was no possibility of anything more between them. She just needed to use the method of delivering bad news she felt most comfortable with— that was, speaking like an attorney, cold and devoid of emotion, but not unnecessarily hurtful.

"Let's just not talk about it, okay?" she said.

Trent made a light choking noise, but when she looked to him, his expression was flat and unreadable. It was silly and adolescent, but part of her wanted him to fight. However, Trent remained silent.

She was glad he didn't say anything, because then she'd feel compelled to debate him. It was her greatest professional strength—her ability to counter someone's argument—and in relationships, her greatest personal weakness. Better to leave things alone for now before he realized he'd grow tired of her.

Yes, they couldn't be together. There was nothing about them that was simple—except in the bedroom, but sex was supposed to be easy. She was of the opinion that relationships that fit into a person's life easily and seamlessly were the kind of relationships that were worth having. If things were a struggle, then it was a case of a square peg in a round hole.

To love was to be vulnerable to the biggest cause of suffering of all—loss.

For now, the best thing she could do was focus on the case and not the future.

Without question, now that she had met the senator, she couldn't deny he should have been sitting in a jail awaiting his trial. She hadn't met his criminal defense attorney, but she had probably been more than well compensated for getting him out on bail, even though the crime and his personal wealth should have warranted remand. He was a flight risk from the beginning. And now that he hadn't appeared, the defense team was probably ready to kill him themselves. They had to have told him, in no uncertain terms, that if he desired any chance of being acquitted of all charges, then he would have to be on his best behavior.

Now, even if he did turn himself in, they would be walking into a trial with a strike already against them. From personal experience, those were the kind of trials she loved to take. She had a reputation to uphold, one that included a ninety percent conviction rate for the state. That was fifteen percent better than any of her colleagues. Statistically, if she kept it up, she was on the fast track to run for District Attorney within the next five years.

"Light's green," Trent said, motioning at the traffic that was already heading their direction.

"Oh yeah, right," she said, pressing the gas pedal

just a little harder than necessary and sending the truck speeding forward. Her cheeks warmed.

"If you want, you are welcome to run me back to my place. Or you can just let me out here," he said, motioning toward the sidewalk. "It's not too far from where I parked, and I can go get my truck."

Though she was sure she should have let him go, she couldn't bear the thought of being alone. "I was actually just thinking about his attorney. I need to give her a call."

There was a sad smile on his lips, like he had sequestered himself to the friend corner where she had been pushing him.

Trent pulled out his phone and started tapping away. "The Bradshaw Law offices are closed—I think we know why—but I managed to pull a home address."

She frowned over at him. No attorney she knew would have their personal address readily available. "Address for what?"

"As it so happens, she posted on social media."

"And?"

"I wasn't finished." His smile widened. "As it so happens, I saw her house in a picture she posted and was able to pull an address."

"Damn," she said, impressed.

He puffed slightly. "It helps to have friends who are in the trenches." He pressed a few more buttons. "Take the next right and head toward Pattee Canyon."

She followed his directions until they were parked in front of a well-kept house. The place had a manicured lawn, raised flower beds in the front and large flower baskets filled with pink and purple petunias adorning the wraparound porch. The house itself was beige, somewhat unremarkable, but freshly painted with a new asphalt roof. It spoke of money but in a way which wouldn't draw attention—just the kind of home she would have expected.

"Let me think about my approach for a sec," she said, looking at the house and pondering how she would feel if someone brought work to her doorstep without announcing themselves first. She liked using the element of surprise, but the attorney probably had a gun sitting right beside the door; Kendra did.

"It will be okay," he said, waving off her concerns like they were inconsequential. "She probably has couriers running back and forth. Whether or not there was a disaster at her office, she still has work to do."

That she knew. While she could get continuances to put off trials, they could only wait so long before she would have to be in court or in a meeting room working out plea deals. "All I'm saying is that I'm sure two people who are standing on the opposite side of her client's best interests aren't likely to be welcome."

"I'm not saying she will click her heels when she

sees us, but she also won't really know who we are," he countered.

She huffed. "That is, unless she has been on social media today. By now, she has to be more than aware of the fight between you and the senator."

"Oh," he said, sounding like she had just punched him in the gut. "Here, I'll give her a call." Not waiting, he dialed. Even from across the car, she could hear it click straight to a call service. He left his name and his number, but he gave her a look that spoke of the fact he knew he would never be receiving a return phone call.

"So, yeah." She tapped on the steering wheel, weighing their options. "You are definitely going to be our weakest link in trying to make contact with this woman."

"Agreed. But I don't think we should give up now. In fact, I would say it won't hurt anything if you go and knock on the door. I can stay in the car, if you need me..." He held out his hand for her phone, and she handed it to him, unlocked. He put his number in. "Now, if you need me, you can get ahold of me."

He couldn't think that if she was in trouble, she wouldn't have time to send him a message, and as such, his action was sweet but ineffectual. At the thought, she chastised herself. She was searching for weaknesses instead of looking at intentions. He had already proven to her on more than one occasion that, if she needed him, he would come running. The same couldn't be said of any of her exes and barely of her siblings—not that she had ever really run to them in her time of need.

Actually, she couldn't think of a time other than when she had been a child when she had really needed anyone—besides this trip. Even when she'd been working in the family business, she'd been ferociously independent and capable of taking care of herself, even in cases where self-extraction had been a necessity.

Yet it did feel good knowing that he would have her back if she required help.

"If you don't hear from me in five minutes, come inside."

He nodded slightly, but she could see from the tense way he moved that he was afraid. There was no denying that his fear wasn't for himself, but her.

It was getting harder to ignore the pressure in her chest that was growing for him each time he looked at her like he was now. Before she second-guessed her choice in pushing him away, she turned off the truck and opened the door. "Five. Minutes."

"You got it, boss."

She wanted to hate the nickname he used, but given the circumstances, she liked it. The name reminded her that she was the one who was in charge, not her heart, him or her family. There was nothing stopping her from going to the front door of this house and asking the questions that needed to be asked.

Stepping out of the truck, she made her way onto the sidewalk and strode toward the door. She pressed the button on the security camera–equipped doorbell and waited. There was a long pause, and she pressed the button again.

A voice erupted from the speaker. "I'm sorry, we do not accept solicitors."

"I'm sorry to bother you, Ms. Thomas, but my name is Kendra Spade, and I'm here to ask you a few questions about your client Dean Clark." Saying it aloud, she was sure that the woman would, in no uncertain terms, tell her to get off her doorstep.

There was another long pause.

"I am deeply sorry about your colleagues at your office. I had the unfortunate misfortune of finding their bodies." Kendra tried another tactic to get the woman to talk to her.

The microphone crackled. "Yes, I'm aware of who you are. You've been all over the news since you arrived in the state. If you don't mind, I have a few questions for you as well."

That made the hairs on the back of her neck rise. It wasn't a hackle response—rather, one that told her no good would come of whatever the woman wished to ask her.

"I'm sorry for coming to your home. I just wasn't sure of any other way to reach you. We tried to call."

Pause. "We?"

Of course, the attorney would pick up on that kind of misstep. "I'm here with a friend."

"You mean the bondsman who physically assaulted my client in the park yesterday?"

Oh, this chat was going downhill quicker than she had anticipated, though she hadn't really expected much. "I would prefer to have this chat in person, if you wouldn't mind."

If she had been in the woman's shoes, she would have been laughing at her request.

"Unfortunately, I'm not at the house right now. If you'd like, you can come to my temporary office space. It's on 410 East Essex. It's in the Sherman Law Offices. They were kind enough to offer me a place." The woman sounded open to the idea of meeting. "I will be available in an hour."

It wasn't a surprise that the woman asked for time. Just like any good lawyer, Kate Thomas needed to collect her thoughts and get her questions in order before she was put on the spot. Plus, sometimes it helped to slow down the pace when it came to forced meetings; it allowed for the host to gain more of a power position. Time had a way of increasing tension. Even though there had been no real direct confrontation between the women, there was still the game of intimidation in play.

"An hour?" Kendra said, looking at her watch and making a show of thinking about her schedule. "I may have to move a few things around, but I think I can make that work. We will see you soon." She gave the woman and the camera a slight wave and walked away, not waiting for a response—two could play the power game.

Chapter Fourteen

From inside the truck, Trent had been able to tell Kendra had been speaking to someone, but he couldn't make out what she had said. She had a perturbed expression when she made it back to him.

"She didn't let you inside. Not a shocker." Trent had been hoping that something would come of their trip up here aside from making themselves look like stalkers, but he couldn't say he was surprised with the way things had turned out.

"No, it was good, though. She's at her temporary office. We have a meeting with her in an hour." Her words and her facial expression didn't align, but he wasn't sure if he should press or just let her open up to him naturally. She pulled out her phone and started clicking away. "According to the map, we aren't far from the offices."

If he had his way, they would have been spending their downtime wrapped in each other's embrace and taking things between them to the next level, but now to even imagine such a thing seemed like some kind of medieval torture device.

Once, he had been ambling around a museum to kill time on one of his many bounty trips—he couldn't remember where—but he had come across a room filled with all kinds of instruments used during the Dark Ages. He shuddered as he thought about the pilliwinks, or thumbscrews, which at this moment he would have endured if it meant they could go back to this morning, before they were interrupted.

She was tapping away on her phone, and after a moment she looked up. "The senator is on social media right now, doing a livestream. Look," she said, lifting her phone for him to see.

The man was talking animatedly, using his hands to make a point. The captions rolled across the bottom of the feed, and from what he could make out, Dean was talking about the "attack." He had a puffy left eye, like he had taken a hit, even though Trent had never landed a punch.

Trent gritted his teeth. "Are you effing kidding me?" He took hold of her phone, and, trying to ignore the lies the senator was saying about him, he studied the background.

"Oh, I'm sure my family is going to have a similar response. I'm actually surprised I haven't heard from them again."

"If we don't move, we will both be getting the what-for from our kin. Luckily, if we hurry, we might be able to catch up with the senator." He pointed at a sign in the background of the video. "Look, right there. He is standing in front of the Missoula Club. Let's go."

She started the truck, and the tires squealed as she punched the gas. He pointed her in the direction of the Missoula Club that had come to serve as one of the key fixtures in the town—it was where everyone went on Griz football game days and the place locals came to talk about anything of importance that happened in the town.

They weren't far from the place, but thanks to the awkward silence, the drive seemed like it took an hour. Things were tense between them, and they were about to go in to what could turn out to be a den of snakes. He should've been mentally preparing himself, as she appeared to be doing, but he found himself only staring at her.

"About this morning—"

She didn't even look away from the road, and yet her expression puckered and put a stop to his attempt to talk things out.

"Trent, there's no question that I'm attracted to you, but we can't really make anything more happen. Sure, we could have some fun, but we both know how these things work."

It was the first time she'd admitted she was attracted to him. Though he knew she was merely trying to soften up her rejection with a compliment, he couldn't stop himself from trying to convince her they could be something more. "Tell me, how do you think this could work? What do you see happening if we give this thing a shot?" She shook her head as though she didn't want to give even the idea a chance.

"Sometimes the things we need most in our lives are the things we have to fight the hardest to get. If you told me you'd want to do this thing, I hope you know I would fight for you."

"We are both capable, intelligent adults who have had relationships before. You can't tell me that our being together would be a good idea." She looked over at him with the raise of a brow.

"I have had relationships. So have you, but I can't say that I've ever been in a situation quite like this before," he said. "Though, since my divorce I haven't really dated a whole lot, so my experience with women is limited."

"I'm sorry about your divorce. I know how hard something like that can be." She gave him a long, appraising look, but he wasn't sure that she wasn't just trying to avoid his offer by being kind.

"Have you gone through it before?"

"Me?" She touched her chest. "No. I never found anyone who wanted to share their life with me."

"Now, I find that hard to believe. What man wouldn't want to spend a lifetime with you? You are incredible."

There was a pink hue on her cheeks. "You are giving me far more credit than is due. I'm as big a mess personally as anyone else."

"We're all just doing the best we can." He chuckled, and some of the strain between them slipped away with the sound. "Things don't always go as perfectly as I would like in my life, either. In my opinion, people and relationships don't have to be flawless...in fact, good ones shouldn't be."

Kendra smiled. "You say I'm incredible, but I honestly can't imagine why you wouldn't have women all over you. In fact, I bet you do." She gave him a sidelong look before pulling her gaze back to the road.

He laughed aloud. "Yeah, right."

He didn't often talk about his divorce, or any of his relationships—what few there were. He knew it was part of developing a relationship with others, talking about each other's pasts and hoping to find common ground to build a new foundation from, but it made him uncomfortable.

"I've not dated much since I've been single." He laughed awkwardly, thinking about the blonde who had broken up with him after learning how his job kept him on the road. "My last girlfriend was not impressed with my life."

It was uncomfortable admitting that aloud, especially to Kendra.

"You don't seem to have any problems communicating with me," Kendra said, and her smile made his heart skip a beat.

"I can't say we have any problems at all." As he said that, he felt ridiculous. There was a slew of problems and impediments standing in their way. "At least… I don't think that any of the problems we have are because of how we feel about each other."

He was met with road noise.

Just when things were getting better with her. He was so ridiculous sometimes. Even now, when he was chastising himself for saying too much, he still wanted to tell her there were at least a hundred things he found attractive about her, starting with how her mind worked. She was so incredibly smart and capable. He really couldn't imagine being a lawyer who had to go up against her in court; she had to be intimidating as hell up there.

A possibility dawned on him, pulling him from his churning feelings of lust and wanting. "I don't think I really asked you, but are you dating anyone?"

She tapped the brakes, sending the truck lurching slightly. "You have to be kidding me. Are you really asking me that now?" She huffed. "I'm not the kind of woman who would have a boyfriend and then try to seduce another man."

Though he knew it was the wrong reaction, a huge smile erupted on his face. "So, you *were* trying to seduce me?"

"What?" She sounded flustered. "Wait. That wasn't the point I was trying to make."

"Doesn't matter. You said it. It's on record." He

laughed. "Regardless of what you want to call it, it happened. I know you think we can't have a relationship because we are from different worlds, but I don't agree."

"You would hate New York if you had to live there." She waved her hands in the direction of the quaint Western buildings that surrounded them. "If I lived somewhere like here, I would never want to leave."

"I never said I wasn't willing to move or that I loved this place. It's beautiful, but I'm not here for the scenery." He tried to sound at ease with the idea, but in reality, Tripp and their business sprang to the front of his mind before he was even done speaking.

"Regardless, we are putting the future ahead of the present. It's probably silly to worry about who would move where when really you should be asking yourself whether or not you really are compatible with me. I've been honest with you about who I am and what people think of me. Obviously, I'm direct. I know it can come off as brash and rude sometimes, and it can push people away."

He shrugged. "I don't think you're rude. If anything, I appreciate you just addressing things head-on. My ex-wife was notorious for masking how she really felt. I'm good at a few things, but I'm not particularly good at reading minds. It was the nail in the coffin of our relationship—her failure to communicate." He sighed. "I blame myself. I should have been more direct. It's a lot of work having to constantly press someone for answers about what they're thinking and feeling, especially when I wasn't there all the time. Yet, I should have worked harder if I wanted to save us. I didn't, though, and whether or not I want to admit it, I let my relationship die."

She nodded slowly. "I know what you mean. Relationships take two people, and no matter what happens—staying together or falling apart—it's the responsibility of both," she said.

He loved that about her…the fact he didn't have to explain himself to her to make her understand what he was thinking. That he could be so open with her, even though he hadn't known her long. "Have you always been direct?"

"I was never particularly shy, even when I was young. My last boyfriend said he loved that I was straightforward, but it didn't take him long to realize while it was great in theory, it was another thing in practice."

"How is it possible that we've had the exact opposite relationship problems?" He laughed as he looked out at the city around them. The downtown area was bustling with people out walking and window-shopping at the variety of pop-up stores that lined the road.

"I'm never going to be a submissive in a relationship. I want to stand beside my partner."

They stopped to let a person cross the road. "Look," Trent said, pointing at the crowd down the street.

In front of them was a large group of people. Most were standing on the sidewalk, bustling about like they were trying to see someone standing in the doorway of the nightclub in front of them. While he couldn't see what they were looking at, or whom, above the crowd was a large red-and-white '50s-style sign that read Missoula Club.

He hadn't really thought they would catch the senator here, especially given the fact it'd taken them so long to drive over, but it appeared like they were going to have another opportunity to get their hands on the man they so desperately needed to find.

"Before I go running headfirst into this thing, we have to be smart," Trent said. He wasn't always one who was metered in his responses, especially when it came to this kind of work, but he had to protect Kendra and do the right thing by her family even if things between them ended there. Hell, even if they weren't dating, he needed to do right by her.

"What're you thinking?" Kendra asked.

"Honestly, that I don't want to do anything that would upset your family. I don't want to set you back in what little progress you've managed to make with your brother." Trent paused. "I'm sure Tripp doesn't want any more drama when it comes to our business, either."

Kendra nodded. She tapped her fingers on the

steering wheel. "Why don't we call the police on this? I mean, all you need is him back in jail, right? We could keep a watch on him until they arrive and take him into custody."

It wasn't a bad idea. Things had a tendency to go all kinds of sideways when he got anywhere near this guy. "I'll text Tripp and see if he thinks we should call it in." He picked up his phone and sent a quick message about the senator's location with their request.

His phone pinged with a message from his brother almost immediately. It simply read, Don't cause nothing. Hold back.

Trent turned his phone for Kendra to see, but he pulled a baseball cap on like it was his best attempt to conceal his identity. "I guess we have our orders. We need to try to disappear."

She parked the truck a block away, and they made their way over to the bar. They could hear laughter as they approached the crowd. Standing on the step, puffy left eye and all, was the senator. He was holding a microphone.

Always the showman.

Kendra leaned in close to Trent. "This guy could give the slickest politician a run for his money. Can't say he doesn't know how to work the crowd."

"You can say that again." He sighed. "This guy is a real piece of work. I don't know how, given his level of popularity—even considering his current murder charge—the jury is going to convict him."

He hated this man who seemed to always be above the law. Hell, he hated anyone who was. He'd had clients at the bond shop who he'd really thought were innocent of crimes, who were later convicted. And yet, here was a man who was almost certainly guilty, and he'd probably get a slap on the wrist—if he was even found guilty. If anything, it also proved the power of media.

"I never try to give the public too much credit. I've seen some crazy things," Kendra said. "But if there is a good prosecutor, he is definitely going to go down for his crimes."

"We'll see. Clark is a snake. He could wiggle his way out of this thing."

On each side of the senator stood two thick men, each wearing scowls. The men were scanning the crowd as if they were looking for threats. He knew the body language of the predator well. These men were there as bodyguards, and also as a show of strength.

He stepped deeper into the shadows and out of the senator's line of sight. He pulled Kendra back with him.

The senator hadn't been here doing a livestream by accident. He had set this up. Guards and all. Had he intentionally been hoping Trent would come for him again? That kind of game seemed right up Clark's alley.

The guard closest to him was thick-jowled, and his face reminded Trent of a pockmarked wolverine. The man looked familiar, but he couldn't quite place him. More than likely, he was someone they had once bonded out. It happened more often than he liked, running into past clients. From the look on the guy's face as he glanced over at him, the man recognized him as well. His scowl deepened.

The guard turned to the senator, and the man instantly stared in Trent and Kendra's direction, but then he returned to addressing his crowd. "It is a sad day for Americans when we are not safe in our own streets," he bellowed into the microphone. "And when we cannot be provided an adequate trial. Instead, we are hunted down like dogs."

The senator shook his fist in the air like he was morally outraged, but it was nothing more than an act. "The America I knew as a child, one built on equality and a justice system that could be trusted, is no longer the America of my adult life."

Trent's resolve at not making a scene or causing problems for the families dissipated. He stepped out of the shadows, and Kendra tried to pull him back. Shaking his head, he pulled free of her grip. He'd had his fill of this man. He couldn't stand idly by for another second—with or without AJ's approval.

"Do you know what I believe is unjust and morally repulsive?" he yelled, pulling the crowd's attention away from the man. "A senator who touts family values and pulls at the heartstrings of his constituents through manipulation tactics that would make most people cringe."

The crowd opened up in the direction of the senator as Trent spoke. The senator's face blanched.

"Why don't we talk about your using your wife's death to gain votes? Or how about the fact that you had her and your own daughter kidnapped?"

"You need to get him out of here!" the senator ordered. "I apologize to those in attendance today. This man is a nuisance. Just yesterday he attacked me without so much as a warning. Some of you may have seen the video! Don't be alarmed, but he is a danger." The senator pointed at his puffy cheek.

The guards charged toward Trent and Kendra. He was tempted to tell Kendra to run, but that would only make it appear like the senator was telling the truth and he was out to get him. Clark was damn good at using the victim card. Trent couldn't play into that.

"I ask that no members of the public put themselves in harm's way," the senator said, his voice nauseating and cloying.

"Senator, what actually happened to your wife?" Trent countered.

The senator's main guard grabbed Trent by the arm and tried to throw him to the ground, but Trent stopped him with one well-timed jab to the throat. He barely looked away from the senator as his hand connected. As the guard dropped to the ground clutching his throat, Trent regretted having touched the man, but it had to be done. "I'm sorry I had to defend myself. But it is important for the public to know about your role in a murder. Not to mention the fact you didn't appear at your last court date. You are a con man, a bail jumper. You are nothing but scum. These people and all the people who voted for you deserve to know exactly what kind of person you are!" His rage pumped through his veins like lifeblood.

Looking to the guard on the ground, the senator smiled. As quickly as the smile appeared, it was replaced by the look of concern. "I am deeply saddened that you would accuse me of such crimes. I'm innocent in the eyes of the law until proven otherwise. There is no evidence. I did nothing wrong." Tears welled in the senator's eyes as he put on the show.

As Trent was about to counter, a police officer approached him.

Kendra's face softened as she looked to the cop. "I am so glad you're here. This man, the senator, has a warrant out on him," she said, pointing up at Clark.

The officer looked to the senator and then back at them, but instead of moving in the direction she was pointing, the officer stepped closer to Trent.

"Sir, there have been reports of a disturbance.

Did you just hit this man?" he asked, pointing at the guard on the ground at Trent's feet.

Trent's entire body went numb. "What? No… I—" The officer motioned for silence, cutting him off.

"Sir, do you wish to press charges against this man?" he asked the guard, pointing at Trent.

His former client looked up and sent him an evil smile. "Officer, I most certainly would."

The senator was moving along the building's facade, disappearing into the crowd and no doubt running from the justice that should have been served.

In an attempt to save what dignity he had left, Trent turned and put his hands behind his back. There was no fighting to clear up this misunderstanding with the officer. He should have never laid his hands on the guard, out of self-defense or otherwise. He looked to Kendra, and there were tears in her eyes.

This time, they both knew the wrong man was going to jail.

Chapter Fifteen

This would all get straightened out. It had to. Kendra watched as the patrol car drove away with Trent handcuffed in the back seat. His eyes locked with hers, and he mouthed the words *It's okay.*

Okay was the last word she would have used when describing what had just happened. Nothing was okay, and in fact, things were consistently getting worse and more confusing as each minute passed by.

She was equally angry at the police officers who'd ignored her demand to arrest the bail-jumping senator, telling her they had no information on that warrant.

Ha!

She didn't believe that for a second and wondered if Dean had paid off someone to look past his crime. They'd also ignored her description of Trent's fight, despite her willingness to swear an affidavit attesting to his acting in self-defense.

Making her way back to the pickup, she felt her purse, making sure her gun was still inside. If she found the senator, this man was as good as dead. She'd never thought of herself as a killer; it was more her siblings' jobs. Yet she was willing to make the sacrifice for Trent. She wasn't sure exactly what that meant about her feelings toward him, but depending on the perspective it was either wonderful or extremely inconvenient.

Starting the truck and pulling out onto the road, she searched the sidewalk for any signs of the senator. If she just looked hard enough, she could find the man. He couldn't have made it that far. She went one block, then two and three.

This man was from the area. If he didn't want to be found, there was little chance she, an out-of-stater, was going to find him.

The meeting with Kate Thomas was in ten minutes. The last thing she wanted to do was go sit down in a lawyer's office, not with everything going on. Trent needed her.

She wished she could be actively helping him, but until he was processed, there was little she could do. They had driven by the police station on the way to the Missoula Club, so it wasn't too far, but the booking process could be tedious on a busy day. He had to have been freaking out. She would have been— especially given the fact it had all just been a terrible mistake.

She thought of the way he had looked at her when

he'd been making his way to jail. It tore at her heart to think about the injustice that was being done.

While she couldn't say with a hundred percent certainty that the senator was guilty of all the things she'd heard, he was far more guilty than Trent. Trent was a good man with a tough job, one that took a special kind of person to perform. It was strange how he could be so self-deprecating when she could find no real fault in his work. Just like everybody else, he had a job to do—a job that didn't always make him beloved. However, she was in the same boat. Everybody was just trying to do the best they could, all while trying to be the best people they could be—that was, except Dean Clark. He seemed to have made a profession out of toeing the line between morally bankrupt and illegal.

She drove by the police station slowly, looking at the large brick building as though its walls were the only thing keeping Trent inside.

The only way she could help right now was by speaking to Kate Thomas and finding out what she knew. Kendra was an attorney through and through. She loved the thrill of standing in a courtroom and convincing the judge that the defendant was guilty. It was such an incredible thing to feel the energy in the courtroom shift in her favor. Often when the defense attorneys questioned her witnesses, there was a ripple in that energy—and that spark of contention and drama was a feeling she sought and could only find in those moments.

Perhaps it was that competitiveness that kept her going. There was so much drama and so much intrigue, but ever since coming to Montana, she hadn't been able to decide whether her job or this place was more interesting.

She could only imagine what would happen if she stayed here for any real length of time. She'd just been here a few days, and already she had found herself embroiled in a set of deaths and Trent had been arrested—the morning after she'd nearly slept with him.

Trent.

She pictured his brown eyes, his strong shoulders and solid physique. The way he made her laugh— even with everything that had been going on since they had first met... Even though how they met was unusual and she should have been leery of him because of his initial secrets, she'd found that she just wanted to be around him.

She shook off the thought. She was fine. *Independence* should have been her middle name.

She slammed her hand against the steering wheel.

That was a lie. She wasn't fine.

She was at a loss without him.

Stopped at a traffic light, she couldn't think of what to do next. If he had been with her, he would've had some clever idea about where to look for the senator or Marla, but on her own she felt like a fish out of water, a new sensation for her. She was usually confident in her abilities.

It wasn't just that she wasn't from here. The town wasn't that big. Basically it was made up of four zones that she had seen so far, and then a medley of suburban developments. She could find her way around, but the problem was knowing where to start and whom to go after first. She had her family's lawsuit to think about, and now she wanted to help Trent bring the senator in so his family business didn't lose money on the bond.

The light turned green, and Siri told her to turn left—as if the phone itself had known she was in need of guidance. Unfortunately, just because it could tell her how to get somewhere, it didn't mean it would provide her with the answers she so vitally needed.

At the bottom of it all, she just wished she could do something more to help Trent.

It's okay. She could still envision him mouthing those words to her.

He must've known exactly how she was going to feel as he was being taken away. Which meant that he had been worried about her when he should have been worried about himself. He was so selfless.

Driving down the road, she saw a heavyset man walking down the sidewalk with his black Lab on a leash. The man had his back to her, but the way his shoulders were shaped reminded her of the guards.

Were they looking for her?

The thought frightened her. With what had just happened with the senator, she was definitely going to be on the senator's guards' radar. For all she knew, she wasn't the one doing the hunting; rather, they were hunting her. It's what she would have done if she had been in the senator's position. Right now, it seemed as if she and Trent were his biggest enemies. With an enemy, the best defense was often a strong offense.

She had a feeling that was something Trent would have said to her, and the thought brought her some peace.

With a few more turns, she found herself around high-end offices and the start of a residential area. Lush, green maple trees lined the road, casting their shade onto the summer lane.

To her left was a large brick building adorned with white windows and black shutters. The building had a colonial feel, as if one of the Founding Fathers had originally constructed it. It was beautiful, with ivy growing up the brick walls around the front entrance. The building was inviting and a far cry from what she had expected to find when going to meet the senator's criminal defense attorney. On the other hand, this wasn't Kate's office.

After parking, Kendra stared down at her phone. Tripp probably needed to know what happened.

She searched for the number for the bonds company. She pressed call, and a young woman answered on the first ring. "Hello, this is Lockwood Bonds, Emily speaking. How can I help you?" The woman sounded far too chipper for Kendra's liking.

"This is Kendra Spade. I was calling to get ahold of Tripp. Is he available?" She had her hackles raised, but as much as she tried to talk herself down from her annoyance, she found she had no control over it when confronted with this twentysomething-sounding girl who must've worked with Trent nearly every day.

She wasn't the kind to be jealous, but oddly enough, it was undeniable. What did that mean?

"Hold on one moment, hon." Emily sounded one step off from giggling.

The fact that the girl had just called her *hon* set her teeth on edge. If Emily had worked for her, she'd have been fired already. There was a time and a place for a jovial and nonchalant manner, but working in a business that controlled the destiny of its customers was not that time.

The phone clicked, and she was sent to the dreaded hell of late-'80s lobby music. She wasn't sure when Mötley Crüe had gone from being edgy and on the forefront of music to becoming so mundane that it could be played while a person was on hold.

After what felt like ten minutes, Tripp answered the phone. "Hey, what's going on?"

Hearing Tripp's voice, which sounded far too much like his brother's, she felt a lump rise in her throat. Now she was getting emotional, too? What was going on with her?

"Hey, so, your brother was just picked up by the local PD. He is being charged for assault." The words came out like they were weighted and they sank in the air.

"Holy crap, are you kidding me?" Tripp laughed, as if he actually thought Kendra was playing some ill-advised and poorly timed prank.

"No, seriously. We ran into the senator. Things went downhill rather quickly." That felt like an understatement. "Is there anything you can do to get him released?"

She could hear Tripp typing away on a keyboard. "I'm looking at the police scanner data now. The boards are pretty empty. We might get lucky, but I have to make some phone calls. I'll keep you posted."

"Thanks, Tripp, I appreciate it." She could hear the relief in her voice.

At least I'm not completely alone.

The thought reminded her of her family. It was odd, but she hadn't even thought of calling them and instead had chosen to call Tripp. She would have liked to say it was merely an oversight and she would call them soon, but as she thought about dialing, AJ popped into her head. He would be absolutely livid if he heard how everything had been going. It was probably a good idea not to have him in the know—not until everything played out and she was back in control and at the top of her game.

"I gotta say, you must really like my brother." Tripp was still clicking away, and he spoke the words like it was no big deal or even slightly surprising.

"What do you mean?" She kept her voice light, as if she didn't really care, even though she hung on his words.

"Seems to me, your family's lawsuit is probably on hold about now. The senator's lawyers were murdered, after all. You could probably head on home to New York and come back and still be ahead of the ball. Yet, you're choosing to stay here and help us out. You're a busy woman. It must be costing you a pretty penny to hole up in Montana like this. Which could only mean a couple of things."

"My family wanted me here."

Tripp chuckled. "And I know my brother is interested in you—or he certainly seems to be. You're definitely his type."

"What type is that?"

She could feel Tripp's self-satisfied smirk even though he was on the other end of the phone. "He likes a woman who takes charge and pulls no punches. As for my brother, he isn't one who normally hangs out with anyone for more than a couple of hours before seeking to be back by himself. He is a lone wolf, so the fact that it doesn't seem like he's left you alone…well, it's telling me all I need to know about his feelings toward you."

"We are just friends, that's all." She wasn't sure why she said it, but something inside her drove her to want to protect their burgeoning relationship…or whatever it was.

"That's good. Trent needs *friends*," Tripp said, a shard of ice smattered in his words. "And I guess I'm glad there ain't nothing more between you two…considering my brother's got a girlfriend. If for a minute I thought you were into him, I'd have to warn you off. As it is, it would be in your best interest to steer clear of him."

Her stomach dropped. Of all the things she'd thought the man was going to say, him telling her about Trent's love life in a context that didn't involve her came as a surprise. Trent had told her—or at least she thought he had—that he was single. She definitely remembered him telling her about his ex-wife, but that didn't mean that he didn't have a new girlfriend.

"I have to go." She hung up the phone, not waiting for Tripp to speak another word out of the fear that what was left of her heart would be ripped to shreds.

Chapter Sixteen

The steel handcuffs were chewing at his wrists like hungry hound dogs. It wasn't the first time he'd been booked, and it wasn't going to be the last—at least, he solidly doubted it. That being said, this was the first time he felt like he was innocent. He had done a hell of a lot worse and never been caught, so to find himself here sitting on the bench and waiting for them to take his fingerprints was almost laughable. Hell, he would have been laughing if it hadn't been for Kendra.

He couldn't forget that look on Kendra's face after they cuffed and stuffed him. She'd looked absolutely terrified. He would've done anything—or gone back in time and made a whole hell of a lot of different decisions—if only he could wipe that expression off her face. She was far too beautiful to look that scared. From the moment he had met her, she had been nothing but confident. Yet somehow, he had broken her.

He'd never really liked the senator, but now he hated the man.

If he ever found the senator's guards in a dark alley, they would get an ass whooping that they would never forget. When he told Tripp about this, his brother would probably want to tag along just to lay down the hammer. His brother could be one hell of a pain in the ass, but when it came to things like this, he was a good man to have standing at his side.

When Trent got his one phone call—which wouldn't be for a while—he wasn't sure exactly whom he should call: Tripp, a defense lawyer or Kendra.

By now, if he was Kendra, he would've been on the first plane back to the city. She didn't have to put up with his crap. She didn't owe him anything. It was crazy how much they had been playing this delicate game of so close, yet so far. Right now, he was farther away than ever.

He was so angry, he could spit. For just about the first time in his life, he was doing the right thing for the right reasons, and yet here he was paying the price for all his other misdeeds. And, of course, he had been made to look the fool in front of her... Would she even stay?

Kendra definitely wasn't his girlfriend; she wasn't even his lover. Though they had come damn close. He would never forget the way she had felt sitting on his lap, the robe slipping from her shoulder, exposing that little puckered scar. If he hadn't been able to see any part of her but her shoulder, he still would've been harder than pine.

The thought made him squirm on the hard wooden bench. Now wasn't the time or the place to think about Kendra naked. It would lead to some odd questions if his body responded. Though, if he had to guess, there were probably people who enjoyed this kind of thing. He had definitely met a few who would get a rise out of being handcuffed and dominated, but he wasn't one of them. He had to really trust someone to even allow them access to his world, let alone have any real control over it.

The officer who arrested him hadn't said any more than what was absolutely necessary during the booking process. Now he was filling out paperwork on the computer, but he kept glancing over at Trent, making sure he wasn't going anywhere.

The guy should've known better. He would've done about anything just to get out of this place right now, and acting up would have been against his own self-interest. He needed to get back to Kendra. She needed him. He'd seen it in the way she looked at him, and now sitting here, powerless, was far more torturous than anything they could do to him inside the jail.

He leaned his head back against the concrete wall behind him and closed his eyes. He tried to calm himself, reminding himself that Kendra was one of the most capable women he knew, but his heart was thrashing in his chest. If only he had gotten his hands on the senator. At least then he would've known where the man was and if he posed any real threat to Kendra.

So far, the man only seemed hell-bent on taking him down and hadn't even really seemed to notice that Kendra had been with him. It could have been an oversight, or it could have been that the senator didn't even know she was gunning for him. Trent hoped for the latter. If the senator wasn't after her, she stood a chance in getting out of this entire fiasco without too much more going wrong.

Yes, that had to be it. She wasn't in danger. She had anonymity on her side. Hell, even her family's lawsuit was probably moot now, too, since the senator was a bail jumper.

The arresting officer made his way over to Trent. "You ever hear the story about the jackrabbit?" The man looked down at him, but even from where he was sitting, he could make out a thin sheen of sweat on the man's brow. The guy even smelled of sweat, the dank, hormonal kind that came after a long day's work and heavy stress.

They had been in the bucket for about an hour, so he couldn't imagine why the man was sweating so profusely.

"Well, have you?" the officer inquired.

Trent shook his head.

The officer sighed. "My grandmother always told me a story about this one jackrabbit. Lived on my family's ranch in North Dakota."

Given the start of the story, he wasn't sure why the man would've thought he'd ever heard it. However, being snarky and picking a fight didn't seem like the greatest idea when he was sitting here at this man's mercy.

"This little rabbit found itself in our family's barn. Wasn't a bad place for a rabbit. In fact, he thought it was real perfect. He could play all around the combine and big machines and stayed one step ahead of any little predators that liked to look outside the barn. At night, the little rabbit would slip under the door and nibble on the grass around the barn and do what rabbits do."

The man looked at him, assessing, like he was making some odd metaphor about how Trent was the rabbit. The man failed to realize Trent wasn't playing—this wasn't some goddamned game to him.

"Sure enough, one day this rabbit got picked up by a little fox. That fox got it in its mouth and moved to start shaking it about, but lo and behold, that rabbit wasn't alone. Out came another one from the barn. Instead of running or turning back and going back in that barn, that rabbit came charging after that fox, forcing it to drop the rabbit in its mouth." The officer sounded annoyed.

If this guy was talking about them, Trent couldn't imagine who would have already come to his rescue and forced the man to let him go.

"Are you saying you're releasing me?" Trent asked.

The officer crossed his arms over his chest, making him look even wider than he already was. The guy was stocky and thick, and the last thing he would've called the guy was fox-like. If anything, he was more like a tank, thick and blocky, the kind of guy who would have no problem taking any dude to the ground.

"Hold your horses, I wasn't done with my story." The officer smirked.

Trent could see this man was enjoying his little show of power. He didn't totally understand why the guy was going after him like he was. For all intents and purposes, they were fighting for the same side when it came to criminals. Or was this guy trying to warn him about something?

"While that little rabbit and his compadre got away, that fox was smart. Now he wasn't just going after one rabbit, he was going after two. So, he hunkered down and waited. It wasn't a day later that those hungry little rabbits poked their heads out, and he devoured both of them. The only thing he left of them was tufts of fur." The officer bristled with the threat.

So, the man *was* going to have to release him. This couldn't have been the first time the guy was faced with something he felt wasn't right or fair, but if the cop had just talked to him and seen his side of things, maybe he could have helped him to understand that he wasn't the villain here.

He looked at the officer, studying him. The guy was young—if he had to guess, he would've said he was probably about twenty-seven. He was just getting to that age where a person was starting to figure life out, but with figuring it out came a complete lack of humility. Life was just about to slap him down. Trent didn't particularly want to be the guy that was responsible for that with this kid, but his own self-interest had to come first.

"Who told you that you had to release me?" Trent made sure not to smile, keeping his expression neutral in an attempt to keep the kid from reading him.

"Who said anything about releasing you?" the young man countered.

Trent tried to stifle his annoyance. The fellow was just learning the ropes. "What sergeant's on duty today?"

"Why do you care?"

"I'm not sure if you're aware of this, but I'm friends with quite a few of your brothers in blue. In fact, I work closely with most of the men here. Detectives really like me." He tried not to sound full of himself, but the kid needed to know that it wasn't Trent who was playing with fire here.

"It's funny, but every time I arrest somebody, they seem to get some new friends around the department." He smirked again. "So, before you go throwing out any names, you need to make sure that they know I'll be giving them a call."

He was growing tired of this kid's game. "I'm currently working with Detective Baker on a murder case. If you wanted to give him a call, I'm sure he'd be more than happy to come down here and talk to me and explain the situation." He didn't really want the dude to call the detective; he was nothing more than a witness for the man. However, if it sped up the process of getting him back to Kendra, he would pull out all the stops.

The young officer dropped his hands from his chest and started fiddling with the latch on his utility belt. He tapped his fingers on the set of handcuffs in the hard plastic shell, making them rattle. It was almost like a nervous tic.

Finally, maybe they were getting somewhere.

The kid pulled out his cell phone and started tapping away, and without saying anything, he went back to his computer.

Trent smiled; he'd be back to work in no time. He'd never been more amped up to get his hands on a fugitive before.

Trent was tired of men like Dean, the kind who never found themselves staring down the barrel. Instead, they were always the one holding it.

The officer answered a phone call. He turned away, shielding his face from Trent's view, and it made him wonder who exactly he was talking to—if it was the detective or whoever had led him to having the conversation about rabbits.

The phone call didn't last more than thirty seconds, and the kid's hands were shaking as he slipped the device into his back pocket and turned again to his computer.

A few minutes later, the door at the end of the hallway opened, and Detective Baker came strolling out. He looked at Trent and gave him a stiff acknowledging nod before making his way to the office area where the patrolman was standing. They had a quick, hushed conversation.

Detective Baker made his way over to Trent and took out a handcuff key. "Why don't you go ahead and stand up and we can get you out of here," he said with a lift of the hand, motioning him upward.

Trent stood and turned toward the wall, holding his arms out behind him so Baker could take the cuffs off. With a quick flip of the key, Baker removed them and tossed them on the floor in the direction of the patrolman. While Trent wasn't sure what they had said to one another, the toss made it clear the two weren't going to become friends anytime soon.

Trent turned back around, rubbing the red welts on the outsides of his wrists where there had been the most pressure from the cuffs. Though he was flexible, it was amazing how much damage a set of cuffs could do to a fully grown man in a matter of hours.

"Sorry about this," Baker said, motioning him

in the direction of the door from which he had first appeared.

"It isn't your fault. If anything, I should have made more of an attempt to control my temper." He walked beside the detective as they made their way down the hall, but as he neared the desk where the patrolman was standing, he found the kid wouldn't look him in the eye. "I appreciate you helping me out. Thanks."

"Oddly enough," Baker said, "I've actually been fielding a number of calls about you and Ms. Spade today. Sounds like you guys have been up to your knees in crap since I last saw you."

Trent reached up and ran his hand over the back of his neck. "Well, hell. It wasn't like we were aiming to cause problems. We were just trying to do the best with what the world has given us." He gave a nervous laugh.

Baker shook his head admonishingly. "You're just lucky that a pair of reporters caught your little scuffle with the senator's guard on film. Otherwise, there would have been little we could have done to get you off being booked for an assault charge. As it is, after reviewing the tapes, Officer Daniels," he said, pointing in the direction of the kid, "and I were able to conclusively say that you were acting in self-defense and no charges could be filed."

He silently thanked his lucky stars. Maybe Baker had been in his corner all along and he hadn't needed to make the young officer call him in. "So, you talked to Daniels earlier?"

Baker chuckled. "No, but it didn't take me long to get things straightened out after I was told you were here. You and I, we have bigger fish to fry than some little pissant coming after you on what was little more than a miscommunication and you being in the wrong place at the wrong time. Weren't you at the wrong place, Lockwood?" The way he said his name made it clear that he wasn't really asking him a question.

"Yes, sir." He felt like he owed Baker more, but he was sure the favor would come full circle some-day when the man would need him.

"A mistake was certainly made by our teams in letting the senator go, but they are now combing the streets looking for the man. We are hoping we can bring him in on his warrant by tomorrow. Which means, maybe you can…and *should*…keep your head down. There aren't many more strings I can pull for you today."

He nodded appreciatively. "Again, thank you. You know I owe you one—especially if you bring in the senator." He probably shouldn't have said that last bit aloud, but he couldn't help it. He really would owe this man more than he knew if he was to put an end to the manhunt.

Baker scanned his key card and opened the door that led to the main lobby. "Before you go home—

and, I repeat, *go home*—I do need to ask you a few more questions about the scene you found at the lawyer's office. Do you have time to chat?"

He didn't have time. He wanted to get back to Kendra, but he would have to do whatever this man asked. It was primarily because of him that he was standing where he was.

The lobby featured a couple of rows of blue plastic chairs, the kind that looked like those in high schools across America, except these had been welded together. "Why don't you take a quick seat?" Baker motioned toward the chairs, glancing around quickly as though he was looking to make sure that they were alone and out of earshot of anyone who cared to listen.

He did as asked, and Baker sat down in the chair one down from him. There was a strange twitch at the corner of his eyes that made Trent wonder if this was going to be less than a friendly little chat and more of an interrogation.

"What's going on? Did you get a lead on your murder investigation?" Trent asked, unexpectedly nervous. "I'm telling you, you need to start looking into Clark's guards. He is obviously willing to use them to get whatever it is that he is after. Now, I don't know why he would kill—"

"Stop." Baker raised two fingers, silencing him. "I know you have a vendetta against the senator, but just because you dislike the man—"

"It's a whole hell of a lot more than just a vendetta. The guy is trying to destroy my family's business, and he is probably going to get away with it. Lockwood Bonds has been in my family for forty years. I can't let him take us down with him."

"You know," Detective Baker started, his voice low and soft, "in my line of work, what you just said could best be called a motive."

"Motive for what?" Trent asked, put out. "All I want is to get our money back."

"You're a friend. If you weren't, I'd let you keep on talking... But, as it is, I think you need to be very careful about what you say next."

The blood rushed from his extremities and pooled down in his feet as his central nervous system kicked into high gear and deep-seated fear took hold. "What do you mean? Am I being investigated for something? What do you think I did?" The questions came out in a single breath, and for a moment he felt like he was fifteen years old again and his dad had just found out he had totaled the family's car.

"We received some new information about the secretary's and lawyer's deaths. As such, there are a few more things you and I need to discuss." Baker leaned forward in his chair and tented his fingers together, his elbows on his knees. His hands were pointing directly at Trent, which made him wonder if somehow he had become their primary suspect.

Here he had been, feeling all too proud of himself for getting out of the assault charge thanks to his connections in the law enforcement community, when in reality he was being looked at in relation to a homicide. His fingers went numb.

"About you and Ms. Kendra Spade… What would you say is the nature of your relationship?" the detective asked.

Trent was surprised by the direct question; up until now, he'd been asking himself the same. "Baker, you know me and women… They're a mystery."

Baker chuckled. He leaned back slightly, as though he was taking some of the pressure off in his questioning. "You're not the only one who doesn't understand them, Lockwood. I'm just lucky to be married to one hell of a woman. I don't know how you still do the dating thing." Baker sat back and scratched his chin. "I know you and Kendra probably haven't defined the nature of your relationship, clearly, but would you say that you are friends?"

"We haven't slept together, if that's what you're asking." Trent was careful to avoid mentioning the fact that, yes, they were definitely more than friends.

Baker nodded. "Would you say that you're a friend of mine, Lockwood?"

Trent nervously ran his hand over the back of his neck, as though the dead lawyer wasn't the only one who had once felt a noose. "I've called you a friend, and I've helped you through more sticky situations than either one of us can probably count."

Baker smiled. "You're definitely right there. So, given the nature of our friendship, if I were to ask you some questions about Kendra, would you be able to tell me the truth?"

Trent couldn't imagine what Baker would ask that would compromise anything he had going on with Kendra. There was definitely nothing to lie about, other than their rendezvous in the hotel room. Trent wasn't one to kiss and tell.

"I have nothing to hide from you, Baker. You know how I work."

Baker dropped his hands back down to his knees. "You know I'm glad to hear that."

"Fire away." Trent wasn't sure he was really ready for whatever Baker was going to ask, but sometimes it was just better to get it over with.

"Well, like I said, some new findings came to light about the deaths." Baker shifted in the chair. "We did find some spent brass near the secretary's body, and while the fingerprint analysis won't be coming back for at least a week, based on some other items we found in relation to the murders… I have a feeling those fingerprints are going to be Kendra's."

It's impossible.

Kendra wouldn't have had anything to do with those murders. First of all, there hadn't been enough time. Not only that, but he couldn't imagine Kendra being able to take down the lawyer and then hang him. Yet, she had a family whose livelihood was at stake. If it came out that STEALTH actually did have a role in the senator's wife's death and his daughter's kidnapping, it would be the end of them.

Maybe she had known Trent was following her and had brought him to the scene of the crimes on purpose to hide something she or one of her family members had done. It was a nearly perfect alibi.

Up to this point, he had thought Kendra was sticking around to help him find the senator out of the goodness of her heart. However, when he really thought about it, there were few people in his life who did anything out of the kindness of their heart. Had his attraction to her blinded him to her ulterior motive?

On the other hand, she very well may have simply touched the casing when she had found the body. It could have been an accident. He was struggling to make heads or tails of what little the detective had told him. "If her fingerprints are on that brass, there are explanations for it."

Baker's face pinched into a scowl. "That was my first thought, too. She doesn't seem like the kind who would kill anyone in cold blood." Baker paused. "That being said, though, did you notice if she was wearing acrylic nails? Gray or silver?"

Trent thought about holding her hands. They hadn't done it much, but he could remember her fingernails against his skin. "I think she does, why?"

"Do you remember if she was missing one? Or if one had been broken?"

Trent shook his head. "I can't say I ever looked at her hands that closely."

"Well, the next time you see her, you'd be doing me a favor if you paid attention."

"So, I'm assuming you found a broken fingernail on scene?" Trent asked.

Baker nodded. "Not just on scene. We actually found a woman's acrylic nail embedded in the lawyer's neck, almost directly below the rope that was used to string him up. All we have to do is match up that nail and we will know the name of our murderer."

Chapter Seventeen

Kendra was rarely annoyed when faced with the fact that others were just as busy and manically scheduled as she was. However, after she had been sitting in the criminal defense attorney's office for more than an hour and a half, she was about to lose it. The woman had set this meeting, and yet after Kendra had checked in with the secretary in the lobby, the woman had disappeared and she hadn't seen anyone again. It was as if she had been forgotten or intentionally waylaid.

It reminded her that when she got home, she would need to send in a plant to her office to see if things ran more smoothly. If people were being treated like she was here, heads would start rolling.

Taking out her phone, she called the attorney, but there was no answer. She called the office number, and the phone rang not far from her in the lobby at the secretary's desk.

Screw this.

She hung up. Something was going on. She could

feel it. If she stumbled onto another crime scene, she would definitely go crazy. Looking at the secretary's desk, all she could think about was the Bradshaw office where she'd first seen the woman's high-heeled shoes and known she was dead.

Her stomach churned.

She wasn't sitting here for another minute. She blew out of the office, anger and a slight trepidation pushing her forward and out of the damned place.

Getting into the truck, she thought about Trent. If personal favors had been called in, he would've been out of jail by now. Yet, he hadn't reached out. That had to mean he was still inside. And, if he was still inside, he was going to be there overnight.

Hopefully, he was okay. Jail could be a rough place, a world where people were frightened and vulnerable. When shame and isolation came into the picture, people turned either inward or outward. And when they turned outward, it often came out in the form of violence. While she was certain Trent wouldn't be the one causing fights behind bars, she held no doubts he would defend himself if put in a situation that required him to. On that point, he was definitely more than capable of taking down any opponent. He was her protector.

She needed someone as strong-willed as she was. She would just walk all over a weaker man. Mild-mannered men could be sweet and kind, but she knew that while they treated her extraordinarily well, they also bored her.

If this, the time she spent with Trent, was any indicator of what was to come between them, she would definitely never be bored. She smirked, and the silly reaction to the thought made her shake her head. While she needed a challenge, what woman wanted that in a relationship? What was wrong with her?

She'd always thought she was the kind of woman who valued stability and reliability when it came to relationships. Yet she had never thought it was possible to have those things in combination with a man who kept her on her toes. In her experience up to now, all men were either one or the other. Perhaps she had found the last unicorn, or the Holy Grail of men. Or she had found a man who was her perfect fit… someone who perfectly complemented everything she was while allowing her to be her authentic self.

A message popped up on her phone from Tripp. It read, Talked to arresting officer. Didn't make a lot of progress. Keep trying. Making follow-up calls.

She wasn't overly pleased, but at least it was something. The thought of going to the jail to get Trent popped into her head again, but if Tripp hadn't made any real progress, there was no way her showing up would likely have any sort of sway. It was better if she just went back to her hotel.

Besides, as much as she liked Trent and could

imagine having him in her life, he had a girlfriend. She could leave his rescuing up to that woman.

Then again, that was assuming Tripp was to be trusted. She had only just met him, while she and Trent had been talking so much—he'd even admitted he'd been ghosted. Maybe Tripp had misunderstood or something. There were a thousand things that could have gone askew. Or maybe Tripp really was telling the truth.

If and when she saw Trent again, she wasn't sure she would give him what for, or if it was best just to pretend like she didn't know about another woman and let things lie.

She made her way back to her hotel, picking up some Taco Bell along the way. She loved Taco Bell. It wasn't something she would admit to a lot of people, but it was her comfort food. There was nothing better than one of their quesadillas on a bad day.

Her hotel room was quiet. Everything was as she had left it; her suitcase was in the closet beside the white robe. She sat on the couch staring at the robe as she ate her food. She would never look at a hotel bathrobe the same way again. Actually, even though she was more than sure that she wouldn't sleep with Trent, she'd have to make a point of taking that robe home with her. It could be the one positive reminder of Montana.

Though this trip had gone wrong in every way, when she glanced out the window, she was met with the river view. She realized she had started to love this place. It was becoming a respite.

Finishing her food, she undressed and stepped into the shower. The water ran down her back, relaxing her. Right now, everything was in the air. Yet, the next time she talked to AJ, she would be able to tell him things were going their way. Though there were no definitive outcomes with the litigation, she had hope her family was in the clear. How could the senator complain about his character being defamed when he was jumping bail?

Getting out of the shower, she put on the white robe. It carried the faint sense of Trent. The smell was intoxicating, and she closed her eyes as she took him deep into her lungs.

There were many scientific papers on how true desire could be tested based on the level of attraction one felt to a potential mate's scent. In fact, she had even seen it on one of her nerd shows—one of a number of documentaries and YouTube videos about science and technology—on which they performed a blind scent test in which women were asked to rate the scents according to level of attraction. The results were intriguing.

Though the olfactory senses were incredible and one of the best when it came to inducing and recalling memories, it was hard to know if that particular skill set was a blessing or curse when it came to Trent.

Regardless, she doubted she would be close enough to him again to delve too deeply. For now, she could just enjoy this moment, this place and the aroma.

She lay down on the bed and, closing her eyes, she let her fingers lace over her damp skin at the edge of the neck of the robe.

Her robe drifted open. It delicately grazed against her leg, reminding her of Trent's fingers. She could have lived in that moment forever. She untied her robe and let it fall the rest of the way open. Her fingers moved down to her center, and she gasped as she thought about Trent and how he knew how to touch her even in her fantasies. Maybe she couldn't have him in real life, but he could be hers in her dream world. If anything, at least in her dream world there would be no drama and no other women to compete against.

She smiled as she thought about him moving down between her thighs on the bed. She could just about imagine how his tongue would feel on her. Damn, it would've been nice to know how that felt in real life so she could have had that memory to pull from. Maybe he was the kind to run figure eights with his tongue, or perhaps he was the kind who buried his face. She had to guess he was the latter. He was not the shy type. He seemed like a giver.

Her fingers moved faster, and she could think of nothing but him and how he would have felt pressing inside her.

As she grew close, there was a knock on the door. She had no idea whom it could be; the previous time it had been AJ. He was the last person she wanted to see right now, especially since she'd finally found a few minutes to herself.

She tied her robe closed, making sure she was properly covered before she moved toward the door and looked out the peephole.

Standing outside in the hallway was Trent. She gasped as she threw open the door in excitement. "What are you doing here? Did they let you out already?"

He chuckled. "What, did you want them to keep me there longer?"

She shook her head. "Of course not. I just thought that you'd be there at least overnight. Your brother said he tried to get you out but he couldn't make it happen."

A shadow fell over Trent's face. He couldn't have possibly known what his brother had told her. Yet he looked guiltier than ever. As much as she wanted to avoid the topic of him having another relationship, addressing it seemed inevitable. If they were going to move forward, even as friends, she needed to know some truths.

"Come on in." She motioned him inside, careful to pull her robe tighter as he walked by her.

He stepped inside, and she let the door close behind him.

"Thanks." He shuffled his feet as though he was just as uncomfortable as she was at the moment.

If he just told her the truth without her prompting, at least they could move forward as friends. But, if she had to pry out information from him, she wasn't sure he was the man she had assumed.

"How did you get out?" she asked, her voice cracking slightly as she thought of how hard it had been watching him being arrested and loaded into the cop car.

She hadn't realized how much she'd missed him until he was once again in her presence. It was as if part of her was restored and she was whole once more. She hated to think about how she would feel when she would have to let him go when they found the senator…or when their time came to an end.

"The prosecutor dropped the charges. Though I think he may have had a little help in making his decision." He smiled, but the action didn't move into his eyes.

Something was bothering him. As much as she wanted to be direct and push him, he needed to tell her his truth on his own time. "Who pressed for that? Tripp?" She could just imagine his brother finding the guard and strangling the man into submission.

Trent shook his head and looked down at her robe. "Actually, Detective Baker had a hand in it."

She frowned. "Why don't I get dressed and we can

go down to the lobby and talk about this or something?"

His expression of concern deepened, and he stared at her for a long moment. "Okay. It's fine if you don't want me here." He sounded hurt.

His reaction both confused and somewhat annoyed her. He couldn't have really thought that she would stay in the dark forever, had he? "It isn't that." She crossed her arms over her chest, preparing herself for the inevitability of getting her heart broken. "Did you see your girlfriend today?"

He laughed, the sound so loud and out of place that she was taken aback and a little hurt. Why was he being dismissive of her? "What are you talking about? Where's this coming from?"

She frowned, as she tried to read him to see if he was lying, or if there was a legitimacy in his being offended. "I know the truth, Trent. It's okay for you just to admit you have a girlfriend." Her throat tightened as all the fears and thoughts she was having bubbled to the surface. He couldn't have a girlfriend. She wouldn't be hurt or humiliated in this way.

"First, I don't know who you've been talking to, but I don't have a girlfriend. And second, I told you that I don't have a woman in my life, so I don't know why you're questioning me." He stepped closer to her, like part of him was hoping to touch her, but when he looked her in the eyes, he stopped moving.

She wanted to believe him. To give herself completely to him and trust in everything he said, but she couldn't. If he was lying to her… Merely the thought of it made her want to break down and cry. "Trent, people lie to me every single day. You can't expect me to just buy what you're saying." She stepped back from him and moved toward the bedroom where her clothes waited. "Tripp told me you have a girlfriend. So, if you do, just tell me, because if I find out on my own after this conversation and learn that you lied to me, whatever friendship we have is done."

She sat on the edge of the bed. He couldn't see her be weak, and right now her knees were threatening to give out on her. She didn't like it, and she didn't know why she was having such a pathetic reaction to confronting him. She was stronger than this. She could handle asking the hard questions…usually.

He walked over to her and pressed on her knees with his, gently nudging her to open her legs. For a second, she didn't dare move, but when he reached up and brushed her hair behind her ear, she melted into his touch. She opened her legs, and he moved closer to her. He took her face in both his hands and looked her in the eyes. "I have no reason to lie to you, Kendra. And I would hope that you would never lie to me."

Though she was aware he was the one on the spot here, she looked up at him. "I've been honest with you since the first moment we met." She wanted to point out that she was the only one here who had been. Yet she remained quiet.

He nodded, but there was something in his eyes that made her wonder what he was thinking about. She believed him about not having girlfriend, but he was still hiding something.

Leaning in, he took her lips with his. His kiss was sweet and gentle, and his lips tasted of watermelon, like he had been chewing gum on his way over to see her. Which made her wonder if he had been thinking about kissing her and being close. It was probably just a nervous tic, but the thought brought a smile to her lips as he pressed his forehead against hers. "Do you know how beautiful you are?"

She looked away from him coyly. "You don't have to say anything to me you don't mean," she said, her voice sounding airy and breathless.

He moved her chin gently with his finger, forcing her to look at him. "I only tell you what I mean. And Kendra...you are the most beautiful woman I have ever laid eyes on. You are incredible."

She didn't know where this was coming from, but she liked his sweet candor. Reaching up, she took his hands and opened them away from her face. She kissed the inside of his left palm and looked into his eyes. "I know we are different, and I know this might only be a temporary thing, but I can't tell you how glad I am that you are a part of my life. I couldn't have made it through this without you."

He moved to his knees and hugged her. From where he knelt, he leaned down and rested his head on her chest, like he was listening to her beating heart. She soaked it in. Right here, with his skin against hers, she forgot about everything else. This was all that mattered. This moment. Being here. With him. In his arms. Touching him.

He pushed back the robe. "I'm glad to see you were ready and waiting for me," he teased, looking up at her with a playful smile.

"You think this was for you?" she countered, giving him a mischievous grin.

"If it wasn't, then I'm the luckiest man on the planet to have shown up at your door at just the right moment." His smile widened as he pressed back the fabric just a little bit more and exposed the inside mound of her breast. His lips found the exposed skin, and he kissed her slowly, like he was savoring the flavor of her body and the lingering aroma of her shower. "You smell so damned good," he whispered, his hot breath tickling the wetness left by his kiss.

"You know, this is all I've been thinking about. When you got arrested, I didn't know what was going to happen or if I'd ever see you again…" As his lips trailed down her skin, she was reminded of her phone call with Tripp. As much as she didn't want to stop his kissing her, she needed to know the truth. "Trent, why would your brother tell me you were seeing someone?"

"My brother was trying to get under your skin. Don't let him."

Her skin prickled with anger. "Why would he want to upset me?"

"Remember when I told you my brother was an acquired taste?" Trent looked annoyed. "I don't always understand his thought process. But if I had to guess what he was thinking, he was probably trying to help me out by trying to make you jealous—maybe he wanted to see how you would react."

It was strange, and it didn't make her like Tripp, but she believed Trent.

"My only question is—" a large smile took over his face "—did it work?"

"You know, this isn't helping me to like your brother." She scooted away from Trent, inspecting him. There was a light in his eyes that made her no longer need to question anything with him. He wanted her. Not just for sex. If it was just for sex, they would have already been deep into the throes of ecstasy in her bed. Instead, they were actually talking. He was reassuring her. He cared for her.

Looking at him, it struck her how crazy it was that life could change so rapidly. There was no denying that she was falling in love with him. And while she didn't know if he felt the same, she knew what she wanted—all of him.

She pulled at the bow that secured her robe and the tie slipped free. She let it drift from her fingers as her robe fell open. His gaze went to her nakedness. She could hear his breath catching in his throat, and he mumbled something she couldn't quite hear but that sounded like a thank-you being sent upward. He took a step toward her, but she stopped him with a wave of the hand. "No."

The smile on his face vanished. "What?" He sounded utterly confused.

"Take off your shirt." It wasn't a request.

He followed her order and unbuttoned his shirt and pulled it off. Beneath was a white T-shirt.

"That, too," she said, pointing at it. "Then your pants."

His smile returned. As he realized the game, his motions became relaxed. He lifted up the bottom of his white shirt and slowly drew it over the top of his head. Then, reaching down, he unbuttoned his jeans. "What about my boots?" He pointed down at his cowboy boots.

She smiled, knowing he was teasing her. "You can leave those on, if you can get your pants off around them."

He laughed, throwing his head back. Collecting himself, he slipped them off and gently set them on the floor in the corner.

"What? Are you afraid your boots are going to get in the way?" Kendra gave him the raise of a brow. "What kind of gymnastics are we going to do around this room?"

"Excuse me, miss? I don't know what you think is going on here, but I'm not a man who can easily be seduced," Trent teased.

"Well, that's good, because I never wanted anyone who is easy." As she said that, she knew the truth in her words. Whether she liked it or not, everything about this—being with Trent—had been a challenge. "Now, take off your pants."

He did as he was told. In fact, he seemed to enjoy being ordered around by her. Perhaps he had to be so in control with the rest of his life that it was a relief to be with a woman who wasn't afraid to ask for what she wanted in no uncertain terms.

"Now sit." He stepped toward her, and she pushed him down onto the bed.

The robe she was wearing slipped down her arms and fell to the floor atop his clothes. For a long second, she stood there in all her nakedness and let him stare. He reached for her, and she moved into his hands. He cupped her breasts and stared at them as he ran his thumbs over her delicate nubs. She threw her head back as he drew them into his mouth, making her moan.

He reached between her thighs, and her knees grew weak as he felt the folds between her legs. Gently, he stroked at her wetness until he pressed his fingers inside and made it nearly impossible for her to stand. "I have to finish what I started," he whispered, kissing the skin between her breasts. "I want to kiss every inch of you until you are the only flavor on my lips for the rest of my life."

She swooned at his words and the pleasure of his touch as he swirled his fingers around her. He wrapped his free arm around her and gently turned her and helped her lie down on the bed next to him. He slipped between her thighs and got down on his knees. Moving her to the edge of the bed, he kissed the inside of her thigh.

All she could think about was the way his kiss felt on her skin and how badly she wanted him to find her center with his tongue. She lifted her hips as his mouth moved closer to her. He wrapped his arms over her legs, holding her still. His fingers dug into her skin with just the right amount of pressure to mean business, but gentle enough for her to want more.

He ran his tongue on her opening and probed inside her. "Trent." She spoke his name like it had its own set of wings.

His tongue moved deeper, and his fingers spun circles on her. Faster. Slower. He moved upward and sucked on her swollen mound. She gasped as he pulled at her. That feeling. She loved that feeling. This man. This moment.

Stars formed in her eyes, and she could feel the pressure for release building inside her with every passing flick of his tongue and swirl of his finger. He knew what he was doing. There was nothing better than a man who could work a woman without having to be instructed through the course.

"Oh my…good…effing…" She moaned sounds that she didn't even know she could make as the end found her and she succumbed to ecstasy.

This man… He was everything she had ever wanted. No matter what was to come, she wanted him to be her everything.

Chapter Eighteen

It felt strangely natural to be sitting at the end of the hotel bed in the chair and watching her sleep the next morning. She was so goddamned beautiful. Even as confident and powerful as she was, he doubted that she could possibly comprehend how gorgeous he found her. If he didn't know better, he would have thought she was actually a goddess. There was no question that she was almost too perfect to be real, and there was no damned way that he deserved a woman as good as her.

She rustled in her sleep and cracked open one eye. Seeing him, she sent him a tired smile.

"Good morning, beautiful," he said. "When you are ready, there's a Starbucks and a croissant on the nightstand." He motioned to the table beside her.

Her smile widened, and she stretched, letting out a loud yawn. "Have I told you today how sweet you are?" Her voice was hoarse and thick with sleep, making her words that much sexier.

"Babe, I'm definitely not the sweetest one between the two of us." There was no doubt in his mind that he was falling in love with this woman, but he couldn't help the nagging doubts he had in his mind about her role in the lawyer's and secretary's deaths.

He stood up and made his way over to the side of the bed and sat down next to her. There were black shadows from yesterday's makeup underneath both of her eyes, and there was white powder on the edges of her lips from sleep. She would've probably thought herself imperfect, but these little details only made her more beautiful. It was a gift to see a woman in the morning. Hell, it was a gift to see a woman in bed.

He was a lucky man.

He reached down and took her hand in his. He ran his thumb over the back of it gently. With his left, he brushed a stray hair from her face, letting his fingers graze against the soft skin of her cheek. She leaned into his touch and closed her eyes. As she did, he glanced down at her hand. The silver-colored nail on her right index finger was snapped in the middle. The sight made his gut clench as he was brought back to the reality of what might or might not have happened and her role in it all.

"When did you break your nail?" he asked.

She opened her eyes as he pulled her from the gentle playfulness and safety that had been his touch. "I noticed it felt odd when I got off the plane. It might have snapped off when I grabbed my bags, but I don't really know when I lost it." She lifted her finger and ran her thumb against the ragged edge of the broken nail. "I haven't been too worried about it. I'll get it fixed as soon as I get back."

She wasn't exactly rambling, but she was definitely talking more than she usually did, which made him wonder if somehow her broken nail had made her nervous. Then again, she was so hard on herself, and this little imperfection could have been making her uncomfortable since he had pointed it out. That, or she really had had something to do with the murders.

She'd had a motive to kill the guy, but he just couldn't bring himself to believe that she would've done such a thing. It was strange—or maybe it wasn't—but he felt compelled to ask her outright about the broken nail and how it would have come to be located in the man's flesh.

"Did you lose it before your meeting with the attorney?"

She looked down at her hand and tucked it into her palm. "I remember seeing it was gone when I left the ranch, but like I said, I think I lost it before that. I've just been so busy." She paused and stared at him for a long moment. "What is going on, Trent?"

He wanted to ask her straight out about her role in the deaths, but he held back.

If she did have something to do with the murders, maybe she needed a safe place to talk about it.

Maybe she even had a reason that things had gone as they had with the man, a reason she had never expressed to him before. Trent wasn't a cop, so if she did tell him that she murdered the man and his secretary, it wasn't as if it would change what had happened. The only difference would be that he would have become an accessory after the fact. That was, unless he turned her in to the authorities and told Baker what she had done.

He chewed on the thought. He wasn't sure he wanted to be thrust into a position of holding her freedom in his hands, but he had to protect her and help her in any way that he could. Was she really capable of killing those people? He couldn't believe it. If she had done the deed, he needed to know why. And if she hadn't, they needed to figure out if it really was her fingernail that had been found at the scene of the crime.

"Talk to me." She reached over and took his hand in hers. "If you and I are going to be something... something more than sex, you need to be honest with me. No secrets."

There it was, the call to arms.

He wanted it all. All of her. All she had to offer, and he wanted it all to himself.

"Kendra, Detective Baker told me something..." He ran his finger over the edge of her nail. The edge was dulled from wear. "Apparently, they found what they believe was one of your broken acrylic nails under the man's noose."

Her mouth dropped open, and she sat up in bed. "There's no goddamned way."

"That's what I thought, but then I got to thinking about it…"

She gripped his fingers, hard. "No. I didn't have anything to do with their deaths." She sounded breathless and hurt. "What would make me even want to take them out?"

He looked into her eyes, trying to read her and make sure she was telling him the truth. The vein at the side of her neck was pressing against her skin, and he could see how quickly her heart was racing. She was stressed, but that didn't mean she was lying…only that this was making her uncomfortable.

He could understand her feeling that way; he felt the stress, too. He hated drama and theatrics. More than anything, he hated that they had to be having this discussion. Life was never easy, and hell if love wasn't even harder.

"If Bradshaw and his secretary disappear, it sure makes it a hell of a lot harder to continue Clark's litigation—at least that is what the detective is thinking."

"Well, then, he is an idiot. I'm a good enough attorney that I don't need to kill people to win my case, especially one as weak as the senator's. It's just a defamation case anyway—hardly worth breaking a nail over, let alone killing someone for." She spoke wildly, throwing her hands in the air.

"I know, but there is nothing more damning than physical evidence."

She deflated, and her hands fell into her lap. Dropping her head, she rubbed the space between her eyes. "You're right. I know you're right."

They had broken her. They had hurt her. Once he found out who *they* were, he was going to kill them.

"Who would want to kill these people and pin it on you? It had to have been someone who could get close to you without you noticing."

"Why do you say that?" she asked, looking up.

"They had to have been watching you. Saw you break your nail. Picked it up and planted it. I don't think they intended on hanging the attorney, but they went with it when the opportunity to plant your nail appeared. If anything, I bet they didn't intend on the secretary being there. That was a fast kill, but she had time to get out of her seat...like she was going to run. They shot her, then went after the lawyer."

"Don't you think the lawyer would have heard the shot and come running out of his office?"

Trent tapped his fingers on his leg as he thought. She was right. There was no way the lawyer would have sat still. "He had that second ligature mark on his neck. Someone had to have strangled him first, then hung him."

"And you have to know, there's no way I could have lifted him."

Trent nodded.

"Then again," she started, rubbing her face once more, "I'm sure there could be some kind of circumstances, counterweights or whatever, that a prosecutor could use against me. It all depends on what the scene presented. Bottom line...this doesn't look good, Trent."

He chewed at the corner of his mouth.

"Please tell me that you don't think I had anything to do with this. Really," she pushed, but her expression was pained, and he could tell she was nearing her breaking point.

"I don't think you did, Kendra. Not only are you not the type, but I just don't see how you could have made it work." He paused for a moment. "That being said, though, I do think it's possible that your family could have set you up to take a fall."

She sucked in a long, audible breath. "I... My family and I, we have our problems. There is no denying that our relationship is contentious, but I don't think they would do that to me. We are a fighting unit, and if they wanted to take me down or hurt me, there have been any number of other opportunities throughout the years."

"I know, but you would make one hell of a scapegoat in this situation. If they were responsible for those murders and are setting you up, it wouldn't surprise me at all."

She sat up from bed and took a long drink of coffee, like it was some magic elixir that could make all the confusion and stress drift away. *If only life was that easy.*

Standing up, she made her way to her clothes and slipped into her jeans, doing a little butt jiggle before zipping them closed. It was amazing how something so seemingly inconsequential could be such a damned turn-on.

"I'm tempted to run out to the ranch and talk to AJ and see if there is any validity to what you are thinking. I mean…" She looked over at him. "I can definitely see where you are coming from with this. Sure, my family wanted Bradshaw out of the way…" She paused. "I just can't see them killing him and trying to pin it on me, though. My family is more of the type that, if there is *collateral damage*, the bodies would likely just disappear and no one would be the wiser."

She slipped her shirt on over her head and then pulled her hair back into a ponytail. She moved to the sink and mirror and scrubbed her face before she dabbed on touches of makeup. As she worked, she kept glancing over at him.

"Does it make you uncomfortable if I watch?" he asked, not wanting to bug her.

She shook her head. "If you've seen me without

makeup and you are still around, I guess you can watch the magic it takes to make me beautiful once again." She smiled, brilliantly.

"You are always beautiful."

Her hands stopped moving, and she walked over to him and gave him a quick kiss on the lips.

As she moved back to the mirror, he had an idea. "I know Baker wanted to talk to you. Let's head him off and be proactive. Show him you have nothing to hide. That will help him to see you're not guilty and get him moving in another direction while he waits on forensics."

Kendra nodded. "Good idea. I don't want to have anyone breathing down my neck any more than necessary. And you know I have no problems answering any of his questions."

His only fear was that if they did see Baker, it would go downhill and she would end up arrested, just as he had been the night before. They didn't need any more jail time between them, or any false charges. They'd have to be smart about this. He knew she was a powerful attorney familiar with all the legal traps a suspect could fall into, but she was emotionally involved with her client—herself—and that could skew her actions.

Finishing up, she grabbed a sweatshirt, and they made their way out of the hotel and to the pickup. Getting in, he dialed the detective.

"Hello?" Baker answered his phone on the first ring.

"I'm with Kendra, and we were hoping to meet up with you this morning, if you have time." He wanted to add that she hadn't had anything to do with the murders and that they were going to prove it one way or another, but he stopped himself. The detective was going to be picking apart everything he said or didn't say, so he needed to be careful about his words.

"Right now, I'm just heading over to chat with some witnesses from last night's little run-in with the senator. If you'd like, I'll happily meet up with you afterward. I do need to ask you both a few questions."

Trent nodded. "We will be more than happy to answer anything you have for us."

"Great, let's meet up at the Double Front Café for lunch. We can sit down and talk. One o'clock?"

"See you soon." Trent hung up the phone and peered over at Kendra. "Did you hear that?"

She nodded. "Let's go see if we can track down the senator." She put the truck into gear, and they made their way out of the parking lot.

He didn't bother to ask her where she was taking him; he trusted her, and he loved the fact that she was happy to lead this fight. She pulled out her phone and fired off a text while sitting at a red light. "AJ is going to have my ass about this, but I have to tell him about the nail. If he finds out from anyone else, I will have hell to pay."

There was no doubt that she didn't think her family was in on this, especially if she was telling them about the murder investigation. If she felt so strongly that her family didn't have a role in this, then he would have to trust her judgment.

He was hoping that she wasn't mistaken.

Her phone pinged, and she sent another text. After a series of pings and texts, she threw her phone down on the console between them as the light turned green. "You keep saying your brother is a piece of work—well, I'm coming to the conclusion mine isn't a whole hell of a lot better." She sighed. "Let's just send them both out to some deserted island without any way to communicate. The world would be a better place."

He laughed as she smiled over at him. Though he knew she was kidding and she loved her brother down to the bone, he could definitely understand how she was feeling.

"What did he say?"

"AJ said he is taking point on this. Apparently he thinks we aren't doing enough, and that's why I am finding myself in trouble here. He didn't want to hear anything in my defense. Needless to say, he is a little amped up. I can't stand it when he gets this way. He is in a full rage."

"Well, he is definitely a type-A."

"They are a special breed, and anyone who is consistently around them deserves a medal," she said, laughing. "Don't get me wrong, I love him and I love my family, but he does drive me up a wall sometimes."

She parked the truck in front of a large brick building. "The senator's criminal defense attorney is working out of this office. She blew me off yesterday. Today I'm not going to give Kate the chance. She, more than anyone, may have a line on where to find the senator. At the very least, we can maybe get her to talk to the man. I've been thinking about it, and he will probably be only too happy to throw us Marla in order to get us off him. I want the defamation case thrown out the window, your bail money returned and this jerk in jail. And any information he has on the murders would be nice, too."

"After last night, this isn't just about the money to me anymore." His anger rushed back as he touched the bruise on his wrist left by the cuffs.

She nodded. "This guy needs to be brought to justice—and be taught a lesson. He's been getting away with crimes for far too long and using everyone around him to skirt the law." She sent him a vicious grin. "I promise you, though, babe, I'm not going to stop going after this man until he pays for his crimes."

She stepped out of the truck and waited for Trent to follow her. Slipping her hand in his, they walked into the brick building and climbed the stairs up to the law offices. A woman was sitting behind the desk in the lobby. She looked up as they walked in and sent them a warm smile. "Hello, how can I help you?"

There was something about the woman that seemed familiar. He tried not to stare at her as he struggled to place the woman, but he found it a challenge.

"We are here to see Kate Thomas. I had a meeting with her yesterday, and unfortunately it didn't quite work out." Kendra sounded civil, but there was annoyance in her tone that made even him feel like he'd done something wrong.

The secretary's eyes darkened, and her entire demeanor shifted, as if she was closing herself off. It made him wonder how much she had to do with Kendra being stood up. "Let me call her, see if she is available. She has been exceedingly busy."

Oh, he didn't doubt that. The woman had to be elbows-deep in all the crap the senator was bringing into everyone's lives.

Kendra moved around the desk as the secretary picked up her phone. "Actually, we are just going to make our way down there. I'm sure she will understand."

"No! You can't go back there." The secretary stood up, but as she moved to stop Kendra, Trent stepped between them.

"No, we are going to let her handle this." He put his hands up, but the secretary moved to step around him. "I said *no*." He blocked her advance with his body. "You just need to sit down, right there." He pointed at the secretary's chair.

"I'm calling the police."

"Perfect. We've already talked to them," he said, shrugging as he followed Kendra down the hall.

Baker is going to be pissed, but screw it. Kendra comes first.

She rushed to the last office on the left and opened the door. Looking inside, she covered her mouth with her hands and turned to Trent, shock on her face. He closed the gap and moved beside her.

Sitting inside the office, across the desk from the female attorney, was the senator. Beside the con man was Tripp.

"What in the actual hell is going on here?" Trent was instantly pissed as he tore into the office.

Tripp stood up and moved closer to Trent. "Hold up, bro." Trent paused, shocked, and without another word, his brother's fist connected with Trent's kidney, dropping him to the ground with the cheap shot. Pain rattled through him. His brother knew how to land a damned punch. He wheezed as he tried to get back up to his feet. Tripp leered down at him. "Stay down, damn it. You know I've got you whooped."

Trent put his hand on the edge of the desk and staggered to his feet. "Not hardly. I was just catching my breath." He moved to swing, knowing full well that even if he landed the punch, his brother was right.

He could count the number of times he'd beaten Tripp on one hand, and those times had only been on the nights his brother was about knock-down drunk.

"Stop. Right there." Kendra had a gun and was pointing it at Tripp. "If you lay another finger on Trent, I will pull this trigger."

Tripp tipped his head back with a laugh. "We all know you ain't got the balls. You may be some high and mighty big-city attorney, but here you ain't no-body, and you damned sure aren't the kind of woman who knows how to run that gun."

Kendra smirked. "Take another step closer and believe me, you'll find out."

Trent tried to straighten up, but his kidney throbbed and his knees threatened to buckle under him. Tears had welled in his eyes, but he tried to blink the unwelcome bastards back. "Tripp, why did you do it?"

Tripp looked down at him, and his lip curled. "Do you know how much money we lost last year? Nearly two million dollars… I told you I wanted to go into the pawn business and you were against it—you didn't want to make 'blood money' from peo-ple who were coming in to get money for drugs by selling crap that wasn't theirs to sell. That's when I realized we ain't never going to make this business work. All we are doing is struggling from one day to the next and running our asses ragged. All because you don't want to be the bad guy. But guess what? Bad men make good money."

His brother was right—he didn't want to be a bad man…no matter what kind of money it would bring in. "So you sold me out to the worst man of all? You know he killed his wife. He is a low-life criminal, and yet you would choose him over your own flesh and blood?"

Tripp flexed his neck. "If you hadn't fallen for that little slit," he said, pointing at Kendra, "you might have seen this coming. You and I know we haven't been getting along for some time. The senator can make things happen for me and our family's business with a stroke of the pen."

"Why did you send me after Kendra if you had no intention of ever bringing him in?" He was so hurt and confused. "What about the money he owes us?" The pain of his brother's betrayal inflected his voice.

"Got you out of my hair for a few days before I worked out the final deal with the senator here." Tripp smirked. "And that money ain't nothing but water under the bridge as soon as you're gone."

Dean started to move toward the door, but Kendra pointed the gun at him. "Sit your ass back down. The police will be here in a minute."

"If they are on their way here, it isn't me who needs to run," the senator said, putting his hands up as he stopped moving. "You're the one with a gun pointed at a senator."

"You know, Clark, you can threaten any number of people and perhaps make them do what you want, but I'm not one of them," Kendra said, her finger moving down to the trigger. "There is nothing I would like more than to put a round in you."

"I'm sure that's true, especially since you have to cover up your role in my civil attorney's death." Clark sneered.

"You and I both know I didn't have anything to do with that," she spat.

"Oh, really? Just wait until they check the security cameras at Bradshaw's office. I'm sure that they will see you shooting that poor secretary. Unfortunately, there isn't a camera in the attorney's office... He really took entirely too long to die." Clark looked from Kendra over at his attorney and sent the woman a malevolent smile. "You know, you two look a little bit alike. Isn't that right, Kate, my love? Very convenient."

The attorney walked over to him, and Clark slipped his arm around the woman's back. "Be quiet, Dean," she said, her voice just one step above a whisper.

"Your love?" Trent choked on the name like it was shards of glass. "But you're his lawyer."

She smiled. "I am. And, Trent, you're not the only one who can have an alias. It is convenient when signing for bonds—especially when the bondsman is on your side and is willing to help you cover your tracks."

He rarely worked under an alias, but of course his brother would have told her that on occasion he would. He had never hated anyone, not even the senator, as much as he hated his brother right now. Tripp had knowingly let Kate Thomas sign as Marla, and then he'd pretended he didn't know her.

Trent moved closer to Kendra, his kidney and back throbbing in pain, but he refused to let it control him for another second. "You are all going to jail."

Clark looked over at him, bloodlust in his eyes. "You will never have to worry about that." He moved his arm from behind Kate, and in his hand was a snub-nosed revolver. He pointed it at him.

The cylinder started to turn as Dean pressed on the trigger. It was crazy how slow time moved as he watched the *click, click, click* as the cylinder moved into place and the round moved into the chamber and waited for the hammer to strike.

As Kendra pushed Trent out of the way, a shot rang through the air.

Trent waited for the rush of fire from the bullet ripping through his flesh. Waited for the pain. Yet, nothing came.

Dean's finger was still on the trigger, but the revolver wasn't fully cocked. Blood was beginning to seep from a wound at the center of Dean's chest. He turned the gun toward Kendra. Another shot rang out.

Dean slumped to the floor, the gun slipping from his hands and falling on the floor.

Kate moved to pick it up.

"Don't you dare," Kendra seethed. "I'd be more than happy to take down an attorney like you—you give us all a bad name. Just give me an excuse to pull this trigger, please…"

The woman stepped back and raised her hands.

"Drop your weapons!" Baker's voice sounded from down the hallway, accompanied by a cacophony of footfalls Trent assumed were from other officers.

Kendra set her Glock down on the ground and raised her hands, sending Kate a vicious smile. "I will see you in court."

Tripp put his hands up in the air.

The police officers burst into the room, Baker at the front of the team. The detective rushed to Dean, who was lying motionless on the floor. He dropped to his knees and pressed at the senator's neck. Baker's face pinched, and he looked at the officer who had come in behind him and shook his head, slightly.

The senator was dead.

Finally, justice was going to be served and evil would be eradicated—but Trent had never imagined his brother was one who had fallen on the wrong side of the spectrum.

Chapter Nineteen

Two months later

It had been a nice break while it had lasted. Kendra
hated the idea of going back to the city, but work
and life there waited for her. She had done as much
as she could remotely, and she had gone back and
forth three times from Montana between making
statements to the courts and meeting with the in-
vestigating officers.

Baker had gone above and beyond in working
with her in clearing her name. The fingernail had
been the hardest part to explain—but thanks to
Baker, she had been cleared when Baker had gotten
Tripp to confess to having found it. He hadn't been
sure it was hers, but had taken it and planted it in an
effort to muddle the murder scene.

From banking records and depositions made by
the remaining Bradshaw employees, they discovered
Brad and Kate had been arguing about the manage-
ment and handling of the senator's cases. Kate had

a contentious relationship with the man—especially when he refused to make her a partner in the firm. Unfortunately, the secretary had been collateral damage.

Love could be a cure, or it could be a curse—and in the case of Kate and Dean, it had led to more deaths and mayhem than even she could have imagined when she had first set foot on Montana soil.

Kendra stared out at the river as it flowed through the back stretch of her family's ranch. Trent was standing in the water near the bank, his arm moving forward and back as he sent out his cast. Watching him fly-fish was like seeing a ballet in the city; there was a beautiful grace to the way he worked the line over the sparkling, nearly translucent river, twisting and turning and letting his line drift to the surface with a series of gentle waves.

She had tried to let him teach her how to do it on her last trip, but after three lost flies, she had handed his rod back to him.

Picking her way down the rocky path to the river, she stopped to the left of him and waited for his line to settle on the water and for him to meld his line before she spoke. "Trent, I need to head to the airport."

He moved toward her. As he did, he smiled, and the simple action pulled at her heart. How could he smile when her heart was breaking over the thought of leaving him?

"Are you sure you have to go? The fish are biting."

His smile widened, but all she could do was stare at his oh-so-kissable lips…lips she wouldn't be seeing for another three weeks.

Stepping out of the water, he put his rod down on the bank and reached down to the pack against his chest.

"Babe," she started, "this is getting harder every time I have to leave you." What she didn't want to say was that she wasn't sure how much longer they could keep doing this before one of them made a change—she couldn't keep coming back here as she was. Yet, she couldn't think of a future that didn't involve this man.

"I know…" His smile faded. "It's not getting any easier for me, either." He pulled out his phone. "That's why I got a ticket for New York. This time, I'm coming with you."

She rushed to him and wrapped her arms around his neck. He took her in his arms and lifted her off her feet as he looked up at her. "I love you."

Putting her hands on each side of his face, she looked into his eyes. "I love you, too." The words she really wanted to say rested on her tongue, but she was unsure if she should say what she was feeling.

"What's on your mind?" he asked, lowering her to her feet but not letting her go.

"I'm thrilled you're coming this time…"

"But…"

She gave him a sad smile. "But I want it *all* with

you. I want you to move to New York. To be a part of my everyday life. I want you to live with me…"

His smile reappeared, and there was a sweet, mischievous glint in his eyes as he reached back into his chest pack. "Well, Miss Kendra Spade, if we are going to live together… What if we were engaged?" He lowered to his knee and pulled out a blue Tiffany's box.

This man knew her favorite color. He clicked open the lid. Inside was the most beautiful diamond solitaire she had ever seen.

"Will you marry me?"

Through it all, she hadn't shed a tear, but looking at him, she felt a single drop slip down her cheek. This man, this incredible, badass man, was on his knee for her. He was her present, her future…her everything.

"Yes, Trent, I will marry you."

He reached into the box and, taking out the ring, slipped it onto her finger. As the cool metal touched her skin, she was warmed by the sensation of forever.

* * * * *

WE HOPE YOU ENJOYED
THIS BOOK FROM

◆ HARLEQUIN

INTRIGUE

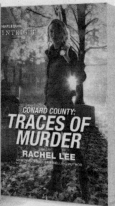

Seek thrills. Solve crimes. Justice served.

Dive into action-packed stories that will keep you
on the edge of your seat. Solve the crime
and deliver justice at all costs.

6 NEW BOOKS AVAILABLE EVERY MONTH!

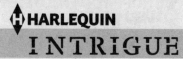
#2097 COWBOY JUSTICE AT WHISKEY GULCH
The Outriders Series • by Elle James
Outrider security agent Parker Shaw and his trusted equine and canine sidekicks are dedicated to safeguarding those in need. Having escaped abduction and imprisonment, Abby Gibson is hell-bent on rescuing the other captives. Trusting Parker is her only option. As danger nears, their choice may come down to saving themselves...or risking everything to save the hostages.

#2098 THE LOST HART TRIPLET
Covert Cowboy Soldiers • by Nicole Helm
Zara Hart is desperate to save her innocent sister and needs the help of her ranch's new owner. Undercover navy SEAL Jake Thompson knows he can't get involved in a murder case. But he *won't* let Zara lose her life searching for justice.

#2099 DEAD ON ARRIVAL
Defenders of Battle Mountain • by Nichole Severn
After barely escaping a deadly explosion, Officer Alma Majors has one clue to identify the victim and solve the case: a sliver of bone. But it's going to take more to expose the culprit. Bomb expert Cree Gregson will risk everything to protect his neighbor. Protecting his heart may prove more difficult...

#2100 MONTANA WILDERNESS PURSUIT
STEALTH: Shadow Team • by Danica Winters
Game warden Amber Daniels is tracking a bear on AJ Spade's ranch when he finds a hand wearing a sapphire ring—one he recognizes. A desperate rescue mission makes them learn to trust each other. Now they must work together to save themselves *and* a missing child.

#2101 CAPTURED ON KAUAI
Hawaii CI • by R. Barri Flowers
To discover why a fellow DEA agent was murdered, Dex Adair and his K-9 are undercover at Kauai's most beautiful resort. And when its owner, Katrina Sizemore, receives threatening letters, Dex suspects her husband's recent death might be connected. Is there a conspiracy brewing that will put a stop to Dex and Katrina's irresistible passion—forever?

#2102 ESCAPE FROM ICE MOUNTAIN
by Cassie Miles
When Jordan Reese-Waltham discovers her ex-husband's web of deceit, she must rescue her beloved twin sons. Her destination: ex-lover Blake Delaney's remote mountain retreat. The last thing she expects is for the former marine to appear. But with enemies on their trail, Jordan's reunion with Blake may end as soon as it begins...

YOU CAN FIND MORE INFORMATION ON UPCOMING HARLEQUIN TITLES, FREE EXCERPTS AND MORE AT HARLEQUIN.COM.

HICNM0822

Parker pulled his truck and horse trailer to a stop at the side of the ranch house and shifted into Park. Tired, sore from sitting for so long on the three-day trip from Virginia to Whiskey Gulch, Texas, he dreaded stepping out of the truck. When he'd stopped the day before, his leg had given him hell. Hopefully, it wouldn't this time.

Not in front of his old friend and new boss. He could show no weakness.

A nervous whine reminded him that Brutus needed to stretch as well. It had been several hours since their last rest stop. The sleek silver pit bull stood in the passenger seat, his entire body wagging since he didn't have a tail to do the job.

Parker opened the door and slid to the ground, careful to hold on to the door until he was sure his leg wasn't going to buckle.

It held and he opened the door wider.

"Brutus, come," he commanded.

Brutus leaped across the console and stood in the driver's seat, his mouth open, tongue lolling, happy to be there. Happy to be anywhere Parker was.

Ever since Parker had rescued the dog from his previous owner, Brutus had been glued to his side, a constant companion and eager to please him in every way.

Parker wasn't sure who'd rescued who. When he'd found Brutus tied to that tree outside a run-down mobile home starving, without water and in the heat of the summer, he'd known he couldn't leave the animal. He'd stopped his truck, climbed down and limped toward the dog, hoping he wouldn't turn on him and rip him apart.

Brutus had hunkered low to the ground, his head down, his eyes wary. He had scars on his face and body, probably from being beaten. A couple of the scars were round like someone had pressed a lit cigarette into his skin.

Parker had been sick to find the dog so abused. He unclipped the chain from Brutus's neck. Holding on to his collar, he limped with the dog back to the truck.

Brutus's previous owner had yelled from the door. "Hey! Thass my dog!"

Parker helped Brutus into the truck. The animal could barely make it up. He was too light for his breed, all skin and bone.

The owner came down from the trailer and stalked toward Parker barefoot, wearing a dirty, sleeveless shirt and equally dirty, worn jeans.

Parker had shut the truck door and faced the man.

The guy reeked of alcohol as he stopped in front of Parker and pointed at the truck. "I said, thass my dog!"

"Not anymore." Parker leveled a hard look at the man. "He's coming with me."

"The hell he is!" The drunk had lunged for the door.

Parker grabbed his arm, yanked it hard and twisted it up between the man's shoulder blades.

"What the—" he whimpered, standing on his toes to ease the pain. "You got no right to steal a man's dog."

"You had no right to abuse him. Now, I'm taking him, or I'm calling the sheriff to have you arrested for animal cruelty." He ratcheted the arm up a little higher. "Which is it to be?"

The drunk danced on his tiptoes. "All right. Take the damned dog! Can't afford to feed him anyway."

Parker gave the man a shove, pushing him as he released his arm.

The drunk spit on the ground at Parker's feet. "Mutt has no fight in him. The only thing he was good for was a bait dog."

Rage burned through Parker. He swung hard, catching the drunk in the gut.

The man bent over and fell to his knees.

Parker fought the urge to pummel the man into the dirt. He had to tell himself he wasn't worth going to jail over. And that would leave Brutus homeless.

"Touch another dog and I'll be back to finish the job," Parker warned.

The drunk vomited and remained on his knees in the dirt as Parker climbed into the truck and drove away.

Brutus had lain on the passenger seat, staring at him all the way to the veterinarian's office, unsure of Parker, probably wondering if this human would beat him as well.

That had been three months ago, shortly after the removal of Parker's leg cast and his move to the Hearts and Heroes Rehabilitation Ranch.

The therapists at the ranch had been hesitant to bring Brutus on board. They eventually allowed him to move into Parker's cabin after he'd spent a three-week quarantine period with the veterinarian, had all his vaccinations, worm meds and was declared free of fleas.

Parker reached out and scratched Brutus behind the ears. In the three months since he'd rescued the pit bull, the dog had gained twenty pounds. He'd learned to sit, stay, roll over and shake.

More than the tricks, Brutus had helped Parker through therapy. Their walks got longer and longer as both veteran and pit bull recovered their strength.

Parker stepped back from the truck and tapped his leg, the signal for Brutus to heel.

The dog jumped down from the driver's seat and sat at Parker's feet, looking up at him, eager to please.

"Parker Shaw," a voice called out from the porch of the ranch house.

Parker looked up as Trace Travis stepped down and closed the distance between them.

The former Delta Force operator held out his hand. "I'm so glad you finally arrived. I was beginning to worry you had truck or trailer troubles."

Don't miss
Cowboy Justice at Whiskey Gulch *by Elle James,*
available October 2022 wherever
Harlequin Intrigue books and ebooks are sold.

Harlequin.com

HIEXP0822

Get 4 FREE REWARDS!

We'll send you 2 FREE Books plus 2 FREE Mystery Gifts.

FREE
Value Over
$20

Both the **Harlequin Intrigue®** and **Harlequin® Romantic Suspense** series feature compelling novels filled with heart-racing action-packed romance that will keep you on the edge of your seat.

YES! Please send me 2 FREE novels from the Harlequin Intrigue or Harlequin Romantic Suspense series and my 2 FREE gifts (gifts are worth about $10 retail). After receiving them, if I don't wish to receive any more books, I can return the shipping statement marked "cancel." If I don't cancel, I will receive 6 brand-new Harlequin Intrigue Larger-Print books every month and be billed just $6.24 each in the U.S. or $6.74 each in Canada, a savings of at least 14% off the cover price or 4 brand-new Harlequin Romantic Suspense books every month and be billed just $5.24 each in the U.S. and $5.99 each in Canada, a savings of at least 13% off the cover price. It's quite a bargain! Shipping and handling is just 50¢ per book in the U.S. and $1.25 per book in Canada.* I understand that accepting the 2 free books and gifts places me under no obligation to buy anything. I can always return a shipment and cancel at any time by calling the number below. The free books and gifts are mine to keep no matter what I decide.

Choose one: ☐ **Harlequin Intrigue**
Larger-Print
(199/399 HDN GRA2)

☐ **Harlequin Romantic Suspense**
(240/340 HDN GRCE)

Name (please print)

Address   Apt. #

City   State/Province   Zip/Postal Code

Email: Please check this box ☐ if you would like to receive newsletters and promotional emails from Harlequin Enterprises ULC and its affiliates. You can unsubscribe anytime.

Mail to the **Harlequin Reader Service:**
IN U.S.A.: P.O. Box 1341, Buffalo, NY 14240-8531
IN CANADA: P.O. Box 603, Fort Erie, Ontario L2A 5X3

Want to try 2 free books from another series! Call 1-800-873-8635 or visit www.ReaderService.com.

*Terms and prices subject to change without notice. Prices do not include sales taxes, which will be charged (if applicable) based on your state or country of residence. Canadian residents will be charged applicable taxes. Offer not valid in Quebec. This offer is limited to one order per household. Books received may not be as shown. Not valid for current subscribers to the Harlequin Intrigue or Harlequin Romantic Suspense series. All orders subject to approval. Credit or debit balances in a customer's account(s) may be offset by any other outstanding balance owed by or to the customer. Please allow 4 to 6 weeks for delivery. Offer available while quantities last.

Your Privacy—Your information is being collected by Harlequin Enterprises ULC, operating as Harlequin Reader Service. For a complete summary of the information we collect, how we use this information and to whom it is disclosed, please visit our privacy notice located at corporate.harlequin.com/privacy-notice. From time to time we may also exchange your personal information with reputable third parties. If you wish to opt out of this sharing of your personal information, please visit readerservice.com/consumerschoice or call 1-800-873-8635. **Notice to California Residents**—Under California law, you have specific rights to control and access your data. For more information on these rights and how to exercise them, visit corporate.harlequin.com/california-privacy.

HIHRS22R2

HARLEQUIN
PLUS

Announcing a **BRAND-NEW** multimedia subscription service for romance fans like you!

Read, Watch and Play.

Experience the easiest way to get the romance content you crave.

Start your **FREE 7 DAY TRIAL** at
<u>www.harlequinplus.com/freetrial</u>.